DEATH COMES RIDING

When a simple job turns out to be a death ride for Lucas, he's rescued by Daniel Brooks, a half-Cheyenne, and Lucas's life is changed forever . . . In the midst of an impending war between the tribes of the Black Hills and the army, Daniel helps Lucas find the men who'd robbed and shot him, leaving him for dead. Meanwhile, Iris Ducane has captured Lucas's heart, but Captain Bagot, from the nearby fort, would kill Lucas to win her hand!

Books by Terrell L. Bowers
in the Linford Western Library:

BATTLE AT LOST MESA
THE GUNS AT THREE FORKS
WARRICK'S BATTLE
A RECKONING AT ORPHAN CREEK
THE KILLER'S BRAND

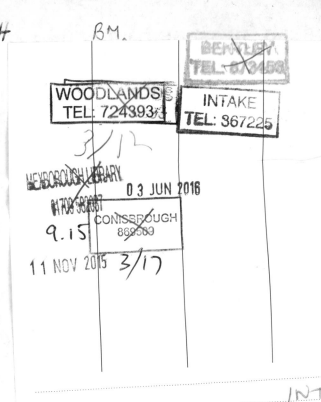

TERRELL L. BOWERS

DEATH COMES RIDING

Complete and Unabridged

LINFORD
Leicester

First published in Great Britain in 2009 by
Robert Hale Limited
London

First Linford Edition
published 2010
by arrangement with
Robert Hale Limited
London

The moral right of the author has been asserted

British Library CIP Data

Bowers, Terrell L.
   Death comes riding.– –
   (Linford western library)
   1. Western stories.
   2. Large type books.
   I. Title II. Series
   813.5′4–dc22

ISBN 978–1–44480–320–4

Published by
F. A. Thorpe (Publishing)
Anstey, Leicestershire

Set by Words & Graphics Ltd.
Anstey, Leicestershire
Printed and bound in Great Britain by
T. J. International Ltd., Padstow, Cornwall

This book is printed on acid-free paper

1

Paveve'keso — Pretty Bird — was awakened by war cries and belated warning shouts. She threw a hasty look toward the camp and immediately grabbed up her baby. Sioux warriors were attacking the small party of Cheyenne! The two braves and her mother were already caught. If she did not act at once, she would also fall victim to the hostile raiders.

Fortunately, she had bedded down a short distance from the others so the baby would not disturb them during their sleep. Only being hidden from sight had saved her from being spotted. There was no time to grab up belongings or the cradle-board. Pretty Bird slipped on her moccasins, hugged the child close to keep him quiet, grabbed a blanket and crept silently into the shadows of early dawn. She went around each bush, careful not to disturb the leaves, hunched low and moving as quickly as she dared.

She heard excited voices and knew the Sioux had found her bed. They would be searching for her. Capturing the wife of Mestaehotoa'e — Ghost Bull — a Cheyenne chief, would have been a great prize. She began to run, fleet of foot, but encumbered by trying to keep the baby from making a fuss which might be overheard.

The death cries of the party she had left behind echoed in the still morning air, but Pretty Bird could not think of their suffering. She and her baby had to escape!

★　★　★

The first glimmer of daylight was upon the world when Lucas topped the knoll overlooking the glen. There was a small pond of water below, surrounded by trees and fronted on three sides by ravines. It was a good place to find the meat he needed for the next few days.

Easing forward slowly, he had the bow and arrow ready for instant use. Not that he favored the Indian style of hunting, but this land was traveled by many tribes. Ever since the incursion of gold seekers into the Black Hills, the number of unfriendly Indian bands had greatly increased. The Northern Arapaho, the Cheyenne, the Sioux — often at war with one another — they now had a common enemy in the white man. Traveling through country occupied by so many hostiles, he would only use a gun as a last resort. Better to go hungry than to fire a shot and alert a nearby band of hostile Indians to his presence.

The crackling sound of branches being disturbed drew Lucas's attention to the adjacent ravine. Sure enough two bucks — a four-point and a spike — were making their way to the waterhole. With no breeze, he knew they would not pick up his scent. And while deer had a great sense of hearing, their eyesight was not so keen as to distinguish a hunter readily from the surrounding brush . . . not if he remained stationary and partially hidden. They stopped at the base of the gully to look and listen. After a few moments, the pair again began to move.

Being a hundred yards away, he needed to get closer to make an accurate shot. He began to ease his way carefully down the hill, crouching and stalking the pair like a wolf. As expected the deer had come to drink. Once confident the pool was safe, they strutted out into the clearing as if there wasn't a hunter within a hundred miles. Reaching the water's edge, the young bucks chose to drink from the side nearest Lucas's position.

Congratulating himself on having picked the best place from which to approach, Lucas edged closer. The deer had their backs to him, drinking their fill. In another few feet he would be in range. Yes, sir, he would have venison aplenty for a week!

Lucas stopped next to a squat juniper and readied his shot. Both bucks had their tails pointed in his direction. He waited for one of them to turn enough to give him a broadside target. Slowly drawing back the arrow, he took careful aim. Any second now, he would . . .

The two bucks lifted their heads as one, suddenly startled. Before Lucas could get a clear shot, both deer sprang into action and bounded away.

'What the hell?'

Lucas cursed his bad luck, but knew the futility of trying to run down a startled deer. Remaining stationary, he used the eyes of a hunter — quickly seeking and finding movement — to perceive what had frightened away his game. Someone with a blanket wrapped around head and shoulders was scurrying down a hill on the opposite side of the small vale. He stayed hidden, waiting to get a look at the person who had ruined his perfectly mapped out hunt.

The sun was not up yet, but the

shadows had receded with the approach of the coming day. It allowed Lucas to see the intruder clearly as he reached the base of the slope and started across the open ground. Staggering uncertainly, as if near exhaustion, the figure in the blanket fell to its knees. As the incomer threw aside the blanket, Lucas saw the new arrival was a squaw with a child. She struggled to her feet and hurried to the pool, where she set aside her baby long enough so she could drink a few swallows of water.

Lucas had seen a good many Indians, even shared his camp with a small hunting party of Shoshone one time. He did not know their languages but he could recognize some of the different tribes. This squaw wore the dress and beadwork of the Cheyenne, not presently a friend to the white man.

'So why are you out here alone, little mother?' he wondered aloud. 'And what are you running from?'

A moment later his question was answered. Three Sioux warriors appeared at the crest of the hill. One spied her and let out a whoop. The trio raced down the slope, following the same path as their prey.

The mother grabbed up her baby and splashed through the pond, frantic to escape. It was a useless gesture. She was carrying a baby and the braves were as fleet on foot as the deer which had left the glen moments before. The woman and child were doomed.

Lucas didn't wish to take sides in a petty feud between two tribes. Indians had been raiding and killing one another since long before the first white trappers appeared. They battled over territories, horses, hunting grounds and for most any other reason men of all colors and races chose to fight.

However, this woman had a baby. To Lucas's way of thinking, no war of any kind should ever include harming or kidnapping an innocent child. The woman managed only a short way before she fell, remaining on the ground, too fatigued to continue. She rose up to a sitting position, defeated, cradling her child in her arms and awaiting her fate.

Lucas raised the bow, drew the arrow back and took aim.

The lead warrior stumbled and went down without a sound. The other two ran past him, but one saw the arrow's shaft and cried out a warning. Even as the second was turning around to see what had happened, Lucas let loose his second arrow. At less than fifty steps his aim was deadly and the second brave sank to the ground as well.

The last man standing had only a war lance and the knife on his hip. He had no idea if he was facing one enemy or a dozen. He ducked low and searched the hillside, scanning for the shooter.

Not wishing to alert the rest of the hunting party, Lucas reached up to the back of his neck and located the handle of the Bowie knife he kept strapped to his back. If he could get close enough, he would kill the third man without alerting any of his nearby friends.

However, the brave chose survival over valor. He whirled about and took off at a full run. His speed was such Lucas could not have hit him, even had he been carrying a third arrow. He hoped it was a long way back to friends and a horse, or he might be up to his neck in hostile Indians in a very short time.

Lucas moved out from his cover and approached the woman. She was still gasping to catch her breath. When she saw him, she pulled her child close against her breasts and shrank back, her expression one of terror.

'Easy there, little mother,' he said gently, putting away the knife and then lifting his hands to show he intended no malice. 'I'm willing to help you, but I sure don't want you to stick a knife in me the first time I turn my back.'

The fear abated from her face to be replaced with a curious frown.

'I don't speak your tongue,' he said, 'but I just killed two of those men chasing you.' He indicated the dead

Sioux warriors. 'I'd say you can trust that I'm a friend.'

'Freend,' the woman repeated, as if she understood the word.

Lucas held the bow in his left hand so he reached out with his right, offering to help her to her feet. To his surprise, she only hesitated a moment, before reaching out and taking hold of his wrist. He pulled her up and pointed.

'I've a horse over the hill. Do you understand . . . horse . . . pony?'

'Poonee,' she repeated and again bobbed her head.

Without another word, Lucas led the way and the woman followed. He had to move slowly, for she was weak and jaded from her escape. She grunted a time or two, while going up the steep slope, but refused his offer of help and did her best to keep pace with him.

Reaching his horse, Lucas was at an impasse. He knew the woman would not want him to ride with his arms around her, but she had a baby to transport. If she was on the back of the horse, she might fall off when he crossed some uneven country.

He decided to leave it up to her. He patted the saddle and looked at her. 'You ride here?' Then he patted behind the saddle, 'Or here?'

The woman was no dummy. She glanced downward at the baby and appeared to take a deep breath. 'Heer,' she said, indicating the front position.

Lucas decided communicating was not going to be as hard as he had thought. He helped her aboard and took up the reins. Before mounting up, he paused to scratch his mare's head from her forelock down on to her forehead.

'I'm sorry, girl, but you have to pack double for a spell,' he told the horse. 'I'll give you a treat and a good rest at Tolberg's post.'

He gave her a final rub, threw the reins over her neck and moved to the side of his animal. Once he had unstrung and tucked away his bow, he swung up behind the Indian woman.

11

She flinched as he reached around her, but he was able to get the reins in one hand and start his mount moving.

'I don't know where to find your home or people,' he spoke to the woman. 'There's a trading post not too far from here. You might know the place — Hank Tolberg is on pretty good terms with most tribes. He speaks some of the Indian tongues and will help us figure out how to get you back to your people.'

She did not respond and he decided she likely had not understood a single word he'd said. Fortunately, she did not object to the direction he chose so he was satisfied with that. Guiding his horse through the lower hills, one certainty stuck in his head. He had to find a way to get the lady returned to her people before either a Cheyenne or Sioux war party came looking for his scalp.

2

Iris swept the hard-pack dirt floor until she reached the door. She paused to step on an ugly black bug which had invaded the sanctity of her uncle's trading post.

'Cross our threshold — you die!' she muttered a posthumous warning.

'You say something?' her uncle spoke up from the counter.

'Yes, I said I'm tired of working every day and seldom seeing anyone exciting.'

Hank chuckled. 'Exciting, says you. We had Indians from three different tribes through here last week, along with two army patrols — both with your favorite soldier,' he gave her a knowing wink, 'and even a small wagon train. Mayhaps I don't know the meaning of the word *exciting*.'

She paused from her chore and a simper brightened her face. 'All right,

Uncle, I'll admit that it's always less boring when Captain Bagot shows up with his troopers. I believe the captain is right taken with me.'

'I would never trust one of them soldier boys,' he complained. 'They are here today and off to way-the-hell-and-gone tomorrow. Loving a soldier is like tying your heart strings to a tumbleweed.'

'But he's a true gentleman, Uncle. He hails from Louisiana, from a fine and wealthy family. Well, they were before the war. He told me they still have a sizable plantation.'

Hank snorted his disapproval. 'His family fought for the South.'

'Louisiana is considered a southern state, Uncle. It was pride for his homeland, not slavery, his family fought for.'

'A proud Cajun Frenchman,' he snorted again, 'like I never heard of or seen one of them before.'

'He's Creole,' she corrected, 'and a captain in the cavalry, serving under a

Union flag now. That ought to mean something.'

'Yeah, it means he's going to be a damn nuisance until you run him off.'

Iris lifted her chin in defiance. 'He acts a perfect escort and treats me like a lady. That's quite refreshing out here in the middle of cricket and sage hen country.'

'I swear, when my sister passed and I took you in, I didn't know you would draw men like bees to a flower blossom.'

'What'cha 'spect,' she teased, using an exaggeration of his own familiar drawl, 'I'm 'bout the only flower blossom in these here parts.'

'Sure, you mock my words, but I'd prefer you acted as skittish as popcorn on a hot skillet around every one of them soldier boys.' The old gent bore into her with a sharp gaze. 'You keep your options open, because something better is likely to come along.' Feigning a troubled look, 'Personally, I'd be glad to be shed of you, but you need to make a good choice when it comes to settling down.'

'You complain about having me here, Uncle, but I can't imagine you being alone all the time. How did you ever manage before I arrived?'

'Tell you one thing certain,' he said firmly, 'I done had plenty of time for ruminating.'

She laughed. 'You won't admit it, but you were as lost and forlorn as a bummer lamb before I came.'

Hank snorted. 'A bummer lamb! You go spouting about how your ma kept a bunch of sheep and won't be a cowboy come near rock-throwing distance of you.'

'Except for an occasional herd passing through, we haven't had more than a dozen cowpokes stop by since I arrived.' She lifted her slender shoulders in a shrug. 'Besides, I'm not going to marry a cowboy.'

'That so? And what's wrong with a cow hand?'

'Oh, maybe I'd consider courting a

ranch owner or some other man of substance, but I don't aim to end up like Ma.'

'Your pa warn't a bad sort.'

'He died of old age at thirty-eight, Uncle. Ma only lasted another three years before the cold winters, hot summers and the endless work did her in too.'

'Well, I'll tell it to you straight, Iris, you don't always get to pick the person you fall in love with. Sometimes fate takes hold of you and shakes the good sense out of you right down to your marrow bones. Before you realize what is going on, you've done lost your heart.'

Hank had never spoken to her in such a way before. Iris leaned on the broom and studied his face. There seemed a distant look in his eyes, as if a memory of the past had sneaked up to catch him unawares.

'Who was she?' she asked. 'Who stole your heart?'

He jumped, as if he had forgotten she

was in the room. 'Nobody,' he said a bit gruffly. 'I warn't never in love with no one.'

'You've been a bachelor all your life, Uncle, but there must have been someone special . . . someone who stirred your heart. Tell me.'

'A man don't go around blabbing about that there kind of sappy stuff, gal. Word got out and the other gents would figure he wore lace on his drawers and cried every time he heard a sad story.'

'It's not so terrible as all that, Uncle,' she argued. 'Being a woman and your niece, I would like to know you have experienced love in your life . . . even if it wasn't returned.'

Hank obviously didn't want to make a confession, but he had allowed the moment to overwhelm him. He stared off into space, as if collecting a treasured memory and spoke in a whisper.

'Her name was Lola DeClaire — leastways, that was the name she used on stage,' he began. 'I saw her when I was in Denver several years back. She could sing like an angel and when she danced . . . '

The sound of an approaching horse put an abrupt end to his story. Iris looked out the open door, miffed that someone had ruined a special moment. When she spotted an Indian woman and baby, sitting atop a jaded-looking mount, she gasped.

'Who is it, gal?' Hank asked, moving up behind her.

But before Iris could reply, she caught sight of a rugged, bewhiskered rider perched behind the Indian woman. He wore a worn, flat-crown hat with a woven horsehair band, crease at the top, with a wide rim to shade his face. Iris had learned many cowboys called such a hat a John B. She saw little more than that before he swung down and helped the squaw and her child to the ground.

'Jumpin' horny toads . . . Lucas!' Hank exclaimed. 'What the Sam Hill have you been up to?' He quickly stepped around Iris. 'And where did you pick up Pretty Bird?'

The man stood head and shoulders taller than the Indian woman. He was tanned from the sun and wind, somber, with chiseled features and a sinewy build, as if he wrestled razor-back boars every day before breakfast. Dressed in buckskin, with a gun on one hip, he wore shin-high, lace up moccasin boots. Unlike most men who visited the trading post, he ignored Iris and focused his attention on her uncle.

'You know this little mother and child?' he asked, his voice a rich baritone.

'She's the wife of Chief Ghost Bull, over at the twin forks of the Little Blue Creek. He has a small camp and his people keep pretty much to themselves, except for when he rides with Dull Knife.'

'I come across three Sioux braves chasing this gal — sent two of them in search of the Happy Hunting Grounds.'

'Damn, Lucas! Those Indians will be comin' here looking to take my hair!'

'The one who got away doesn't know I'm a white man. I used a bow and arrow to down the other two. Then coming here, I crossed where a herd of elk must have been feeding and mixed in my tracks. I doubt there's any need to worry about them showing up.'

Iris took notice of the woman's haggard condition. 'It looks like the lady has scraped her knees,' she spoke up. 'And the poor thing is probably dying for some food and water.'

The man her uncle called Lucas finally rested his gaze on her. She perceived a glimmer of appreciation, but didn't know if it was because of her concern for the Indian woman — or did he like what he saw?

'I ran out of grub and water last night and didn't take time to stop and fill my canteen. I reckon we could both stand a little food and drink.'

Hank spoke to Pretty Bird — a mix of words and sign — and she gave a nod of understanding.

'Iris, take her to the back and get her

some water — maybe you can do something for her scrapes too.'

The girl stepped up and smiled at the woman, then made a gesture with her hand to have her follow. Pretty Bird did so without hesitation.

'You took a big chance getting mixed up between two tribes,' Hank told Lucas.

'I heard a rumor about a move to unite all of the tribes against the whites, what with the broken treaties and gold seekers moving into the Black Hills.'

'I've heard much the same,' Hank said. 'There's been talk of a big parley between the major chiefs of the Sioux, the Cheyenne and the Arapaho tribes for later this winter or early spring. Some wise old bird, name of Tatanka Yotanka . . . believe the name means Sitting Bull, is trying to bring them all together.'

'Considering what happened today, it would seem they are still doing some bickering.'

'Indian affairs aside, I've been hoping

you would stop by. I was in Crossbow a short while back, picking up a load of supplies. You know how I hate to pay what the freighters want these days.'

'Can't blame them for charging a stiff fee for hauling freight over this way. They are risking their lives coming here, what with a half-dozen bands of Indians looking to kill any white men they come across.'

'Trust you to see it from a teamster's point of view.'

'I *was* one of those teamsters not too long ago.'

'My point exactly.'

Lucas wrinkled his brow at the statement. 'What do you mean *your point?* What are you talking about?'

'I ran into your old pal — you remember Jim Grogan, the American Community Bank manager — the man you *used* to work for?' Lucas gave a nod of his head and Hank continued. 'Well, he's got himself a problem. There's a gent named Martin who wants Grogan's Bank to deliver a payroll . . . up into the Black Hills!'

Lucas laughed without humor. 'Good luck finding someone to do that.'

'Jim has a couple men rounded up as guards, but no one who actually does courier work for the bank wants the job. He asked if you might be interested — claimed the trip would pay three times the normal rate.'

'That's not enough, considering you're paying a man to get himself killed.'

'It would set you up with enough money so you wouldn't have to work all winter less'n you wanted to.'

'Even if I were fool enough to say yes to this idea, how can Jim afford to pay triple wages?'

'Because that there Martin fellow has demanded his money be insured against any loss. If Grogan's Bank don't deliver the payroll or loses the money, they have to pay him back.'

'That's a fool's bet. We're not talking about an exchange between the American Community Bank and another bank or one of its offices. This is a ride into hostile territory where anything can happen.'

'It's becoming a more modern world out there in the big cities, Lucas. A traveling drummer told me about some big hotel what done burnt to the ground back East, and the whole thing was rebuilt because the owner had himself some of that insurance. He claimed the place was built back better'n new!'

'Insuring a building or even a man's life is a lot different than insuring the delivery of a sack of money.'

'Well, I told you about the job. The delivery needs to be made in the next few days, so you still have time to get there, if you decide to take on the chore.'

The girl who had taken Pretty Bird back for treatment returned. She was petite in build, with sand-colored hair and dazzling green eyes. She gave Lucas an appraising glance but spoke to Hank.

'We cleaned and bandaged her knees

— well, I gave *her* the bandages and she did it herself. She drank about a gallon of water and is breast-feeding her baby. I thought I would fix something for her to eat.' She flashed a bright smile. 'What about you, big boy? Didn't I hear you say you were hungry?'

'I had to stop myself from gnawing on the rawhide straps holding my bedroll in place the last coupla miles,' Lucas replied. 'I'd be happy to pay for whatever you prepare for both the little mother and me.'

She smiled again. 'I already put on the taters and cut some bacon to fry up. You want coffee?'

'If it's no trouble.'

The girl displayed a winsome sort of pixie expression. 'Oh, it's trouble,' she retorted, 'but you're going to be paying for it.' Then she whirled about and disappeared into the store.

'What was that?' Lucas asked Hank, giving his head a tilt in the direction the girl had gone.

'That prancing piece of apple-pie

fluff is my niece. Her folks are both gone and I'm the only kin she has in this part of the world. Tell you the truth, she's a bigger handful than anything I ever throwed a loop at in my younger days.'

'This is a heck of a place to have a young woman, out here in the middle of nowhere. What about the roving bandits, dangerous killers and Indian war parties scattered through the hills?'

'Afraid them fellows will have to take their chances,' Hank quipped.

Lucas had to smile. 'I need to put my horse where she can get some rest. I've been riding steady for a week and she packed all three of us for the last four hours.'

'What do you intend to do about Pretty Bird?'

'You still have those two old nags in your corral?'

Hank bristled defensively. 'I'll have you know them are the finest steeds this side of the Kansas City! Either one is worth double the coyote bait you're riding!'

Lucas grinned. 'You don't have to give me a sales pitch — I'm not buying.' With a more serious tone, 'I need to get the lady home before the Sioux come looking.'

'I'll second that notion, son. You can borrow the two mares for the trip.'

'Thanks,' Lucas said, 'at least I can rest easy that no one is going to kill me in order to steal my horses.'

'You keep making rude comments about my steeds and I'll let you walk all the way to the Indian camp.'

Lucas chuckled, but returned to serious business. 'I'd appreciate you having a talk with the little mother about my intentions. I'd like to leave Ghost Bull's camp with my hair intact.'

'Not to mention my two prize horses,' Hank replied haughtily. 'I'll speak to her after we all have a bite to eat. Go ahead and put up your pony and give her a handful of oats — the barrel's just inside the barn.'

'Thanks, Hank. I'll be back in a few minutes.'

* ★ ★

The Indian woman had used the changing cloth Iris provided and placed the baby on the blanket. Iris watched the little tyke as she started the meal simmering. Although he wasn't old enough to crawl, the little boy did enjoy kicking his legs and flailing about with his little arms.

'What's his name?' she asked, pointing at the baby. 'Him, how is he called?'

'Pahketa,' the woman replied. She made a sign with her thumb and first finger and then pointed at a bear skin tacked to the back of the trading post wall.

'Small Bear?' Iris said. 'Little Bear?'

Obviously one of the titles was close enough for Pretty Bird's limited English. She gave an affirmative nod.

'I am Iris,' said the white girl, tapping herself on the chest. 'Iris.'

'Paveve'keso,' the Indian responded. 'Preey Burrd.'

Iris realized at once she would need

to stick to calling her by the English names. She didn't have to speak, however, as Hank came over to join them.

'Pretty Bird,' he said using sign at the same time. 'We are going to eat and then Lucas will take you home to Ghost Bull. You understand?'

'Hoom,' she said, comprehending his words. Then she said something in Cheyenne. It sounded like gibberish to Iris but it must have concerned her rescue.

'Lucas is a good man,' Hank told her, as if in agreement.

'Goo man,' she again attempted to put the words into English.

'Speaking of the *goo man*,' Iris cracked a grin, 'He is exactly what I was talking about earlier. I believe he's kind of' — she cooed the word — 'exciting.'

'Now, Iris, I done told you — '

'You just told Pretty Bird he was a good man.'

'Reckon that's the truth. He's been nothing short of a top hand ever since I met him.'

'When was that?'

Hank thought for a moment. 'I first set eyes on Lucas when he was a younker. I landed a job running a relay station — back in '61 it was — and Lucas rode in, not a day over thirteen years of age. He had hired on riding for the Pony Express.'

Iris was genuinely impressed. 'At thirteen?'

'Even at that age, he was a little older than the youngest rider ever hired by the Pony Express,' Hank replied. 'Small size was the thing that mattered, for the sake of the horse. I recollect Lucas was not more'n a hundred pounds when fully outfitted for cold weather. He rode for us until we was forced to shut down because of the war between the Union and the Confederacy.'

'What else do you know about him?'

'Best get back to the stove,' Hank warned her. 'You burn his meal and he'll be thinking you don't know a table fork from a pitchfork.'

The ready smile flashed. 'Oh, all

right, Uncle. I swear sometimes you're about as closed-mouth as a tripped bear trap.'

He grinned at her analogy. 'Durned if you ain't starting to sound like you belong working here at a trading post.'

'Bite your tongue!' she teased. 'I'm setting my sights a little higher than that.'

Before Hank could reply, two men entered the store. Iris decided, by their dirty and unkempt look, they were either hunters or men on the run from the law. One was fairly tall and lean, while the other was average in height, but sported a hook nose and was a bit cock-eyed. Both wore beaver headgear, were armed with both knife and hand gun and it was evident neither had shaved nor bathed in a long time.

'Shep . . . Skinner,' Hank greeted the pair, having turned to see who had entered the trading post. 'What brings you boys over this way?'

'We're heading for the western part of Colorado until the Indian trouble is settled,' the taller man replied. 'Big war coming to these parts. I hear tell the Utes are more casual about a man doing a little hunting on their land than the hostiles around here.'

'Say!' the other stopped dead, his eyes fixed on Pretty Bird. 'What the hell you got here, Tol?' He elbowed the tall man. 'You see that there Injun, Shep?'

'I see her, Skinner,' Shep replied, his look also growing as cold as ice. 'What are you doing with a Cheyenne squaw in your place, Tol?'

Iris saw the Indian woman stiffen. She placed a reassuring hand on the woman's shoulder and flashed her most winning smile at the hunters.

'You boys hungry?' she asked, moving to place herself between the men and Pretty Bird. 'I've got food cooking on the stove.'

Shep extended a dirty paw and gave her a shove, pushing her aside to get a better look at the Indian woman. 'Damnation, Skinner! I'd wager she's from one of the villages who kilt

Trapper Jed and his family!'

'Wait a minute,' Hank tried to slow the two down. 'This isn't what you think.'

'Stand clear of her, Tol,' Skinner warned. 'Jed was a friend of ours and his Shoshone wife and two boys were butchered alongside of him. It's time for a little payback!'

Iris again moved in front of Skinner, this time taking an unyielding stance and placing her hands on her hips. 'Don't you dare come into our trading post and start harassing our customers!' she scathed the two men with her words. 'This woman and baby have done nothing to you!'

'You being our friend,' Shep growled at Hank, 'you maybe ought to toss a loop on this here feisty kitten and leave us be. We'll take the squaw and her nit outside so we don't bloody up your place.'

'Shep's right, Tol,' Skinner was also incensed. 'We got no quarrel with you. Stay outa' this and you won't get hurt.'

Skinner reached out and attempted to sweep Iris aside for a second time.

'Keep your filthy hands off me!' She shrieked. Before Skinner realized he had blundered into a hornets' nest, Iris flew at him with fists flying, attacking like a rabid banshee!

'Ow!' he cried, as her balled fist struck his nose. He took a step back before he managed to catch hold of her flailing wrists to stop her from hitting him. Iris changed tactics and kicked him hard on the shins. Skinner yelped again and pulled her in close so she couldn't do any more kicking — she ducked her head and sunk her teeth into his forearm.

'Holy hell!' Skinner cried out from pain and turned her loose. Stumbling away from her brutal assault, he threw up both hands for protection. 'Shep! Get her off of me!'

Shep sprang behind Iris and wrapped an arm around her, trying to subdue the girl. She squirmed and twisted in his grasp, then stomped down on his toes. He let out an oath as she whirled about, kicked him hard in the knee and raked her nails along the side of his face.

'Tol!' Shep cried out, throwing up his arms for protection. 'Damn it, Tol! Call off this here she-cat before we have to hurt her!'

'Hey! You two!' a booming voice commanded from the doorway, 'Let the girl alone!'

Iris ceased her attack at once and, as Shep backpedaled to safety, she scampered over to stand behind Lucas, who had entered the trading post.

'What's the idea of coming in here and attacking this young lady?'

'*Lady!*' both hunters exclaimed in unison. Skinner pointed to his nose, which had bled some and held out his forearm to show where blood had also seeped from a set of teeth marks. Shep turned his face to show where Iris's nails had taken three strips of skin from his cheek to his neck.

Lucas flicked a quick glance back at

Iris. Her hair was in disarray and her breasts were heaving from her heavy breathing due to the strenuous exertion.

'They were,' she paused to gasp for air, 'they were going to take Pretty Bird outside,' she panted for air a second time, 'and *kill* her and the baby!' she finished.

'The Cheyenne kilt a close friend of ours and his whole family,' Shep gave the details to Lucas. 'You remember Jed Quigley, don't you?'

'That's right,' Skinner said. 'Butchered him and his whole family. We are only looking to square a debt.'

'Not with my prisoner, you're not!' Lucas stated resolutely. 'I captured her and I'm the one who is going to turn her over to the soldiers.'

The two men exchanged incredulous looks. 'Turn her over to the soldiers?' Shep muttered, as perplexed as if he didn't understand English.

'That woman and baby are Ghost Bull's wife and child,' Lucas informed them. 'Ghost Bull is one of Dull Knife's sub-chiefs. He and his warriors won't join in any raids while the soldiers have his family. I figure those two will earn me a hundred-dollar reward from them boys in blue.' With a hard look. 'If you two fellows want the squaw and her baby, you best be ready to fork over the hundred in gold.'

Skinner waved a dismissive hand. 'Shucks, Lucas, we didn't know the Indian was your prisoner. No one told us you were here.'

Shep bobbed his head affirmatively. 'That's true — we know you're one of us.'

Lucas relaxed his posture, having averted a fight. 'I'm glad we got that sorted out.'

Both Shep and Skinner smiled in agreement.

'I'd admire to remain cordial with you boys,' Lucas continued, speaking easily, 'but I have to ask you to apologize to the young lady here.'

The two men displayed pained

expressions. Shep raised both hands, as if the request was more than he could swallow. 'Damn, Lucas, she's the one who done all the hitting, scratching and biting.'

'Kicked my shins till they're raw!' Skinner added, whining over the notion. 'We shouldn't have to apologize for the damage she done to us!'

But Lucas held firm. 'I've got to ask it, boys. The girl was protecting my property.'

Skinner reached up and removed the beaver hat from his shaggy head. 'I reckon we was a might abrupt, ma'am,' he said reluctantly. 'Me and Shep are sorry for trying to manhandle you.'

'That's right,' Shep concurred. Then reaching up to gingerly finger the scratch marks on his neck. 'Hate to think we might have been less than gentlemanly with you.'

Iris stepped forward and patiently used a hand to move an unruly lock of hair from dangling down her brow. 'Perhaps I should have told you about

Mr Lucas,' she said. 'I didn't realize you knew each other.'

'We've crossed trails on more than one occasion,' Shep told her, offering a toothless smile as a peace offering. 'Even done our share of swapping lies around the campfire on occasion.'

'You need us to ride with you, Lucas?' Skinner asked. 'Might be some of the squaw's people lurking about.'

'Appreciate the offer, boys, but I've got fresh horses lined out. And no one is going to miss her for a few hours yet.'

'Good luck to you then.'

Hank moved over to the store counter. 'Did you fellows need something today?'

'Ammunition and jerky,' Skinner told him.

'Some chew for me,' Shep added. 'Ten plugs ought to be enough.'

The two hunters moved toward the counter, made their purchases and left the trading post.

Iris stepped quickly around and planted herself in front of Lucas.

'You didn't mean what you said?' she demanded to know in a hushed voice. 'You wouldn't turn Pretty Bird over to the soldiers?'

Lucas cast a glance to make sure Skinner and Shep wouldn't hear. 'Not to worry, little wildcat. I'm taking her straight home after we've eaten.'

A mischievous simper appeared, playfully curling Iris's sinuous lips. 'Just so you know,' she murmured in a teasing voice, 'a wildcat wouldn't stand a chance with me, big boy.'

Lucas studied her for a long moment. He was truly captivated by the girl. A simple look into her dazzling sea-green eyes summoned a weakness in his knees and caused a churning in his chest like a full-grown bat was trapped inside and flapping about, trying to get out. The sunflower-blonde hair adorned her face the way an expensive frame sets off a work of art.

'You're looking at me like you're hungry,' Iris teased. 'Somehow, I don't think it's only a meal you're wanting.'

Lucas was dumbfounded by her candor. He had to swallow his fascination before he managed to reply, 'You are the most remarkable woman I ever crossed trails with, that's a fact.'

She raised a single eyebrow. '*Remarkable?* Hmm, is that supposed to be a compliment?'

''Bout the biggest compliment I can give,' he answered. 'You've likely heard all of the usual flattery — given by men with a whole lot more experience around comely young ladies than me.'

His words prompted another charming uplift at the corners of her mouth and it seemed the gold sparkles surrounding the iris of her eyes ignited like fireworks at a county fair.

'You do know that *comely* is a word often used as flattery?'

A second lump of air formed in Lucas's throat blocking the next words he would have attempted to utter. However, Iris seemed to feel their repartee was at an end and took a step back.

'If you're quite through ogling me like a thick, juicy, steak,' she jibed, 'I'll move Pretty Bird into the back storage room and serve her food in there. You can take a stool at the table in the corner and have your meal with me and Uncle Tolburg.'

'Uh,' Lucas cleared his throat, 'Much obliged.'

The girl spun about, her skirt swirling with the motion, and practically minced across the room. She took a few moments to attend to the bacon and diced potatoes before they burned. Then she escorted Pretty Bird into the back room and out of sight.

'Lucas, old buddy,' Lucas muttered, 'there's a woman you could study your whole life and never learn everything there was to know about her.' He smiled. *But it would definitely be great fun trying.*

3

Lucas took a roundabout route to avoid any possible contact with the Sioux warriors who had attacked Pretty Bird's party. Hank had spoken back and forth to the woman and learned she and her mother were returning home from a visit to Ghost's Bull's father. He was quite sick and wanted to see his grandson before he died. Little did he know the journey would cost the lives of Pretty Bird's mother and three braves.

Lucas chose to rest the horses near a major trail crossing. He took a moment to look and listen, making sure all was quiet, then offered his canteen to the woman. She declined, patiently waiting for him to start moving again. He had to give her credit: no matter what the situation, she hadn't asked for one thing since he had rescued her.

It was the way of the Indian woman, he supposed. The men had their hunting or raiding parties to plan and carry out. Being warriors, they would ride horses while the women usually walked. When confined to camp they might plan raids or hunts, play games or sit around and tell stories. For the woman, she gathered berries and roots, collected firewood and buffalo chips to keep the fire fed. She made the meals and chewed the fat from buckskin or scraped buffalo hides to make the material pliable and soft for clothing or moccasins. For her recreation, she made blankets or would dry meat and fish, and all the while, she would raise and tend the children. No question about it, if Lucas had come into the world an Indian, he would have wanted to be born a man.

Minutes passed. Being satisfied no one was nearby and the horses had rested long enough, Lucas started up a narrow gully. The path showed some sign of recent use, so Lucas did not get too far ahead of Pretty Bird. He didn't want the Indians to kill him before they realized Ghost Bull's wife and child were riding with him.

A short way along the wash and the trail entered a wider canyon. The walls were not high, but horses and riders were exposed to ambush from either side. Lucas caught a glimpse of more than one warrior as they began to follow him and Pretty Bird from either ridge. The hair prickled along his arms and neck, knowing he could be killed at any moment.

He anchored his jaw and continued forward, showing an outward boldness he didn't feel. Never before had he ridden into a hostile Indian camp. The sensation of being naked and vulnerable was not a pleasant feeling.

'Man!' Pretty Bird suddenly spoke. He threw a quick look in her direction and discovered she had stopped her horse. He did the same. Before he could question her as to the reason, no less than a dozen warriors came spilling over the hill from either side.

The urge to draw his gun was strong, but Pretty Bird edged her horse out in front of Lucas and waited for the braves to surround them. One Indian seemed to be in charge of the others. Dressed in buckskins, his braided hair dangled well below his shoulders, and a bright yellow headband supported a pair of eagle feathers at the back of his head. He approached and spoke to Pretty Bird. They exchanged several sentences, which meant nothing to Lucas, and then the Indian looked at him.

'White man much brave or much stupid,' he said, a stony expression on his face. 'You want we should kill you now or maybe later?'

Lucas gave him a curious look. 'Is there a third option?'

'That's a stupid thing to say,' the man replied in perfect English. 'How is a poor ignorant Indian supposed to know a word like *option?*'

Lucas smiled. 'You speak better English than me.'

The serious expression vanished and the man laughed. 'My father was a trapper and fur trader. He was fifteen years older than my mother, and I came along when he was near fifty years old. He died when I was about twelve so we rejoined my mother's family with the Cheyenne.'

'My name is Lucas and I found . . . '

The man lifted a hand. 'Know all about it,' he said. 'Pretty Bird told me how you saved her life . . . twice.'

'It wasn't much trouble the second time,' Lucas admitted. He then asked, 'What happened to the uniting of tribes against the soldiers? How come the Sioux raided Pretty Bird's party?'

'I'm sure it was a band of Sioux looking for leverage to trade for weapons,' the man replied. 'We have acquired a number of new Winchester 66 rifles. You might know something of those guns — they hold up to thirteen .44 caliber rimfire rounds. It will give my people quite an advantage over the soldiers, who still carry old single-shot carbines.'

48

'So the Sioux wanted to trade for the guns, but didn't want to give up anything of value,' Lucas surmised. 'They grab Pretty Bird and use her to get what they want.'

The man grinned. 'You have reasoned it out, my friend.'

'With such shenanigans going on, I suspect the bonding between the various tribes is not going to last very long.'

His words prompted the man to laugh. 'You have a point, white man.'

'So what do I call you?' Lucas asked.

'My Indian name is something you probably can't pronounce, so we'll stick with my white name — Daniel Books.'

'All right, Daniel. If you have a horse the lady can ride, I'll leave her with you.'

'For a man of such great courage, I'm surprised you are so eager to run away from a Cheyenne thank you.' He challenged Lucas with a sardonic grin. 'This might be the last time you will ever be invited to an Indian camp . . . unless you are brought in as a captive.'

'Funny, but I don't remember the last time I ever heard of the Cheyenne taking a full-grown man captive.'

The smile broadened. 'You would only be a captive a short time . . . be dead much longer.'

'And you have to ask why I'm anxious to turn tail and skedaddle?'

Daniel grew serious. 'It is good for my people to see a white man who does not wish us all dead. You and I know the future is dark for the Cheyenne, for all Indians.'

'The soldiers are as many as leaves in a forest, Daniel. I fear the time for the Indian to run free as the deer is at an end.'

'What you say is true, Lucas. Ride with us to the camp of Ghost Bull and I promise no harm will come to you.'

Without any real choice in the matter, Lucas gave a nod of his head. 'Lead the way, my half-Indian friend.'

★   ★   ★

Hank returned from his final check on the stock — Lucas's horse, two goats, a sow and five piglets, along with a lame mule and a dozen chickens. He hung his hat on the rack near the door and closed the window shutter.

'You don't think Mr Lucas will return yet tonight?' Iris asked.

'He probably didn't reach Ghost Bull's camp till twilight, gal. Smart man doesn't travel after dark in Indian country.' Hank took a long look at her. 'You ain't setting your cap for that drifter are you?'

'Drifter?' She lifted her chin in his defense. 'You called him a top hand.'

'He don't even have a job right now. I done told him how to earn his keep for the winter months ahead, but a man needs a home, a place of his own, when it comes time to settle down with a woman. You're the one who told me how you wouldn't marry no wandering cowpoke.'

'I don't believe he's wandering at all,' she again took up for Lucas. 'I think

51

he's looking for something better, a place to belong . . . and maybe a wife too.'

Hank placed his hands over his heart and groaned. 'You're gonna sure 'nuff give me apoplexy, gal! I ain't been your guardian for a full season and already you're chompin' at the bit to run off with a captain in the cavalry or a hunter you only met a few hours ago.'

'If it wasn't nearly impossible for a woman to find a job and earn a living for herself, you wouldn't have me here at all. You said it yourself earlier today . . . I'm starting to sound like you! Mother was always correcting my speech or grammar and you're going to have me sounding like a mule skinner!'

'Well, I don't want that Frenchman or Cajun or Creole — whatever the heck he is — to sweet talk you into something you'll regret. I think you can do a whole lot better than to marry a career soldier.'

'He has yet to mention anything about marriage,' she answered back.

'And Lucas is a good man, but he ain't got two coins to jingle in his pocket'

'Yes, I know, Uncle. You needn't worry; I'll make a good choice when I decide to marry.'

'It's getting late,' Hank put an end to the conversation. 'I got to be up early and boil some hides. That's one of the drawbacks to dealing with Indians, they don't always tan or clean the hides before they bring them here to trade.'

Iris uttered a sigh. 'I suppose I can get up early and help.'

Her offer caused him to soften his stance. 'You needn't fret about Lucas, gal. I reckon he'll be back for his horse tomorrow. Most tribes don't kill a man who saves the wife of their chief — enemy or no.'

'I feel so reassured,' Iris said sarcastically.

'You head on to bed. I'll put out the lamps and lock up for the night.'

Iris didn't hesitate. Uncle Hank was a gentleman, but they had to share the tiny bedroom. She would always get into bed first and rise after he was up in the morning. It was the only modest way to change from her work clothes to her nightdress.

Once under the covers, she squirmed to get comfortable on the cot. The bed didn't have an actual mattress, only a couple inches of straw packed tightly beneath a canvas ground blanket, held in place by a four-inch high board railing. Her single luxury item was a feather pillow, taken in trade from a passing wagon train. While the rest of her body might complain about the discomfort of practically sleeping on the ground, she did enjoy the soft cushion for her head.

The final glimmer of light went out and Hank entered the room. She heard his boots being set on the floor and knew he had draped his pants over the rail of his pole-frame headboard. His bed was a bit larger than hers, but he had given her the feather pillow, using one stuffed with cotton for himself.

Iris stared at the blackness overhead and considered her future. It was not very bright presently. Captain Philippe Bagot was smoothly elegant, with a polish about his speech and manner, and he knew many words and phrases to flatter a woman. Conversely, his smugness and arrogance sometimes got the better of him. He could not help being pompous as it was in his very nature. In spite of his faults, he was the only real suitor she had presently. Oh, other men flirted with her, some were quite forward, but few of them were serious about proper courting or possible marriage. They were usually the sort who liked to show off for their friends by trying to induce a poor, attention-starved trading-post girl to swoon at their feet. The majority of men who frequented the trading post were travelers, along with the occasional troopers, miners and cattlemen moving a herd.

She had no interest in most passing through, and it was unsettling to meet a couple men like the two who had wanted to take vengeance on Pretty Bird. Hank had also warned her that a few of the men who stopped at the post were bandits or desperadoes. In summation, she had thought Philippe to be the only adequate suitor until Lucas walked through their door. Now she was torn between the captain and the hunter.

Thinking of both men, Philippe had a habit of looking at her with confidence, as if he expected her to surrender to his charm. Lucas . . . well, he was different. There was a curiosity embedded in his gaze, but also the hint of something more. It was as if he truly enjoyed what he saw, yet he maintained a certain reserve. She had shamelessly beguiled him, calling him *big boy* and teasing him with her eyes. It had been excessive and completely out of character for her, yet she had wanted to make an impression on him. There had been a panic in her soul, as if she was afraid the one encounter might be the only chance she would have to impress the man.

When considering his actions, she thought how rare it was to find someone of his moral fiber. He had not only killed two warriors to save an Indian woman, but had been ready to fight with the two hunters — either friends or acquaintances of his — to keep her safe. And Pretty Bird belonged to a tribe who were currently waging war against the white man. More than that, he had forced the two hunters to apologize to her.

What makes him different than the others? she wondered. Yes, he had risked his life to save an Indian woman and her baby, but there was more to his character than that. She . . . *felt* it. He wasn't an ordinary man. She had a notion Lucas would treat his woman as if she were the most precious gift on earth. Her uncle said he didn't have a real job, but Iris was certain a man like him would make sure his family had a roof over their heads and food on the table. He would love and protect them with every breath in his body. What woman could ask more from her man than that!

* * *

Captain Bagot arrived with a dozen men shortly before noon. He smiled broadly at Iris when he entered, leaving his troops outside with their mounts.

'Ah, my dearest Iris,' he gushed forth with his praise, 'my heart takes flight like an eagle when I look upon your goddess-like features. I would cross a valley of fire to behold your beauty.'

'What brings you over this way today, Capt'n?' Hank asked from across the room, purposely interrupting the man's flattery.

'*Monsieur* Tolberg,' Philippe diverted his attention to Iris's uncle. 'We had a report that there was an Indian woman here of some rank within one of the tribes.'

'An Indian woman?'

'*Oui*, we were on patrol some miles from here and spoke with two hunters,' Philippe explained. 'It was my understanding there was a hunter staying here with a captive to turn over to us.'

Hank moved over to stand alongside Iris. 'I 'spect you're talking about Pretty Bird and Little Bear, the wife and baby of Ghost Bull.'

'*Oui*.' His eyes swept the room. 'Did we miss the man with the captive?'

'There was a slight change of plan,' Hank told the captain. 'Lucas took the woman back to her people.'

The news caused a dark hue to flood Philippe's expression. 'Lucas you say!' He appeared to grind his teeth. 'We have heard of this man, a scoundrel who deals with the Indians, a man who may well be supplying them with rifles and ammunition!'

'Lucas will sometimes trade or give meat or salt to a band of hungry Injuns,' Hank told him firmly, 'but he don't deal no weapons! He knows there's a war comin' and he ain't going to side against his own people.'

'Yet he returned the woman to Ghost Bull!'

Iris jumped into the fray. 'She is the man's wife . . . and she had her baby with her.'

'My dear Iris,' the captain began patiently, 'this is not — '

'Philippe — ' Iris cut off whatever he was going to say, 'Her little boy was only a few weeks old. It would have been morally wrong to separate them from her husband.'

Before he could offer a rebuttal, one of the soldiers stepped into the room. 'Pardon the interruption, Captain,' he said brusquely, 'but there's a rider headed this way and he's leading an extra horse.'

Iris and Hank looked at each other. She immediately suffered a dreadful sensation, fearful of an upcoming confrontation.

Philippe followed his trooper outside with Iris and Hank both on his heels.

Lucas started to ride past the dozen

troopers but Philippe strode out into the yard to block his path.

'You would be *Monsieur* Lucas?'

Stopping his mount and the spare horse, Lucas paused to look down at the captain. 'If you're speaking to me, I don't answer to Cajun French.'

Philippe bridled. 'I am not *Cajun, Mr* Lucas,' he said tightly. 'My father married a Spanish lady of high society. I am Creole French.'

'All right, you're a horse of a different color, so what do you want?'

'I have some questions for you,' he regarded Lucas with a scowl. 'Questions you would do well to answer.'

'Make it short. I been up most of the night, Lieutenant, so I'm a might surly. What is it you want to know?'

'It is *Captain* Bagot,' Philippe corrected haughtily. 'And two traveling hunters informed us you had captured an Indian squaw . . . the wife of Ghost Bull.'

'They were mistaken,' Lucas replied.

Philippe was taken back at the

61

statement. 'You did not capture this woman?'

'No, I *rescued* her from a handful of Sioux. I suspect they were going to ransom her for some new rifles.' He put a hard look on the captain. 'That's something you soldier boys ought to be looking into, where the Indians are getting their guns. If all-out fighting starts, your men are going to enter into battle with outdated war relic carbines, while the Indians will be shooting back with newer model Winchester rifles.'

'Perhaps I should ask you the question . . . considering you are on such amicable terms with the Indian populace.'

Lucas met the captain's accusing stare for a long few seconds before answering. 'I'll say this slowly and clearly, just so there won't be any confusion. I don't deal guns to the Indians. It's always my aim to avoid contact with any of the tribes. I've done a lot of hunting and driven freight for the last few years, but yesterday was the first time I ever entered an actual Indian camp. I was given no choice in the matter, and I parted company as soon as they would allow. The chief wanted to thank me for saving his wife and child — that's what he did — and that's the end of my association with any of the tribes.'

'I can vouch for Lucas,' Hank spoke up, before Philippe had a chance to reply. 'He's been working this territory since the Pony Express was in operation. He ain't going to trade rifles to the Indians. Look at what he carries — an old Henry .44. If he was dealing new guns, he would sure enough own one himself.'

'So why did you tell the two hunters the story about turning the Indian squaw over to us?'

'To keep from having to knock them both senseless — those are friends of mine.'

'She was an Indian,' Philippe said with distaste, 'a savage.'

'She was a mother with an infant in

her arms,' Lucas countered. 'You go making war on women and children — I don't care who they are — you're on the wrong side.'

'I agree with Mr Lucas,' Iris spoke up. 'Pretty Bird could hardly be considered an enemy combatant.'

Philippe cast a sharp glance her direction, as if irked she would intercede during his interrogation. He quickly masked the emotion, but remained serious when he spoke to her.

'There are stories of such seemingly docile Indian women who cut the throats of the very men who helped them as they slept,' he said. 'Do not be too naïve, my little flower. It is nearly impossible to find a noble savage.'

'Almost as hard as finding a noble officer,' Lucas quipped.

Before the captain could object, Lucas started his horses forward. Philippe had to move or be trampled underfoot. He retreated to the front of the trading post and stood next to Iris. Once Lucas reached the corral the captain dismissed the episode. Turning to look at Iris, he put a smile on his face.

'It appears I brought my men here for nothing. We cannot escort an Indian if she is already back at her own camp.'

'She was harmless — frightened and harmless, Philippe.'

'I have a three-day leave coming in a week or so,' he changed the subject. 'I will be calling on you.' He lowered his voice so it wouldn't carry to his men or her uncle. 'We could use the time to get to know one another better. Perhaps a picnic and a nice ride together. We might even make the journey to Crossbow. You could do some shopping and we could eat at the best restaurant in town.'

'Perhaps,' she answered carefully.

The captain returned to his horse. Once aboard, he flashed a confident smile at her a last time and, raising his hand, started the troops moving. They whirled about and went down the trail, lifting up a cloud of dust from the hoofs of the animals.

'Like I said,' Hank's words were sour, 'you can do better.'

Iris displayed an impish smile. 'I think I'll go down to the corral and see if everything went smooth with Pretty Bird's return.'

Hank's retort was deliberately sarcastic. 'Yeah, I wager you probably stayed awake all night worrying something might happen to her and her baby.'

Iris purposely sauntered lightly down the beaten path, knowing her uncle would be watching with a secret smile on his face.

Lucas had unsaddled Hank's two horses by the time she arrived. She waited while he forked some cut grass for them and checked the watering trough. When he exited the corral she was there to meet him.

'Looks as if you still have all of your hair,' she said, eying him closely. 'Don't see any nicks from an Indian lance or arrow and you're still in one piece.' A coy simper, 'And I should add, you're a sizable piece, big boy.'

Lucas could see the girl had a first-rate sense of humor, and her eyes were alive, as brilliant as a readied branding iron.

'I was surprised to discover Chief Ghost Bull had heard of you, Bright Eyes. Some of his braves have been by the trading post and told him about you.'

'There are quite a number of Indians who come in to trade with Uncle Hank,' she admitted. 'I don't know one tribe from the other.'

'Six good horses,' he replied.

She displayed puzzlement. 'Six horses?'

'Yes, his brother-in-law is looking for a bride. He asked if I thought Hank would consider that a fair trade.'

She surmised he was kidding and laughed. 'Well, on certain days, he might think the offer was excessive.'

'Could I trouble you for something to eat?' he turned to business. 'I ate a little at the Indian camp last night, but left early this morning so as to not wear out my welcome.'

'I imagine the chief was glad to see

his wife and child back safely.'

'Yeah, he was, but it won't stop his men from killing me if our paths cross again. That's what war is all about.'

'What would you like?' she asked. 'I was going to fix chili con carne for Uncle and me.'

'That would suit me fine . . . if you have plenty to go around.'

She displayed her most winsome simper. 'For you, big boy, I'll make an extra large portion.'

'You've got about as much spunk as a month old cougar . . . and are twice as cute. Do you flutter your sparkling green eyes at every man who comes along?'

Iris turned sour and drew a bead on him with a rapier stare. 'Are you calling me a flirt?'

He showed a good-natured grin. 'It's the reason I asked the question. I'd like to think you're showing me a special attention, but I wouldn't want to act on the wrong impression.'

'I believe it would take a big rock and

a hard throw to make an impression on a head as thick as yours,' she barked her reply.

Rather than being offended, his smile broadened. 'Good, because I have to admit, you're the most remarkable and charming female I ever set eyes on. If you're going to steal my heart, I'd hope to think you're being straight forward with me about doing it.'

Iris remained steadfast, masking her own feelings. It wasn't a smart move to encourage a man she knew so little about, yet she could not help the way she felt. She wanted this man to notice her — wanted it so much she had behaved shamelessly!

'Are you staying here the night?' she asked, desperate to try and act like a normal person.

'No, I need to get started for Crossbow. Your uncle told me about a job and I don't want to get there too late to take it.'

She couldn't hide her disappointment. 'If you are as smitten by me as you claim, when are you going to find the time to come courting?'

'Just as soon as I finish the job,' he vowed. 'You can count on it, Bright Eyes. A team of mules couldn't keep me away.'

'I'll go and start the chili.'

'That will give me time to clean up and shave,' he told her.

She smiled and said, 'I like a man who is willing to put a little effort into his pursuit.' Then she strode back toward the post, feeling the eyes of the man watching her. She was careful not to exaggerate the sway of her hips, because her mother had always told her she had a pleasant, natural grace to her walk. The reminder didn't stop her from putting one foot slightly in front of the other, which she knew would cause her skirt to swish with a back and forth motion. After all, it wasn't teasing to want Lucas to notice she was a nubile young woman!

4

Lucas got along well with Jim Grogan, the manager of the American Community Bank in Crossbow. The expected new route of the railroad promised the new town would grow to the size of Cheyenne within a few years. It hadn't come to pass yet, and with the Indian problem still looming, it would be some time before anyone started another push for rails. Even so, Jim had connections and was part of a banking empire. American Community Bank had offices from Saint Louis to Santa Fe. They handled funds for the railroad and offered nearly the same services as Wells Fargo did throughout much of the country.

Lucas had stopped working for the company because driving a wagon and transporting valuables wasn't all he wanted to do with his life. He had come within an eyelash of being killed several times and it didn't do for a man to push his luck too often. However, with winter coming on, he was enticed by a single job that would pay enough to get him by until spring.

Jim greeted him like a long-lost relative, shaking his hand until he practically wrung the meat off of the bone.

'Can't tell you how glad I am to see you, Lucas,' he said, finally releasing his hand's iron grip. 'It's been some time.' He looked to one side, as if trying to look over Lucas's shoulder. 'You still packing that humongous Bowie knife?'

'I like to think it covers my back — kind of like having someone watching over you to make sure you stay safe.'

Jim laughed, practically giddy over the relief of having Lucas there to help him out of a serious fix. 'I got to tell you, I'm in a real pinch here,' he voiced the same thought. 'Without your help, I don't know how I would ever get this payroll shipped.'

'Tolberg said you were actually going to guarantee delivery with some kind of insurance?'

'It's a growing trend, Lucas,' Jim told him seriously. 'Insurance is the biggest thing to come along since the railroad.'

'But something like this?' Lucas shook his head. 'You're promising delivery into the Black Hills country, Jim. There are a half-dozen hostile Indian tribes floating around, along with a host of claim jumpers and bandits. The chance of a man getting robbed is pretty steep.'

'Martin has hired two men to ride guard with you. He has promised me that they are both capable with a gun and not afraid of a fight.'

'I prefer traveling alone,' Lucas said. 'I don't want to be watching their backs and trying to do a job too.'

'Listen to me,' Jim said, lowering his voice, as if fearful someone would overhear. 'This job will make us both a fair sum of money. I couldn't offer a typical insurance for something like this. Martin is paying twenty-five per cent to make sure the payroll reaches his mine. He's afraid his men will quit for lack of being paid.'

'How much money are we talking about?'

'Sixteen thousand dollars.'

Lucas took a step back, stunned by the number. 'Sixteen thousand! In cash?'

'Martin will put up four thousand dollars for the insurance. Once you return, I'll pay his two men five hundred each and you a thousand. The company still earns two thousand dollars for the delivery.'

A dozen different warnings sounded in Lucas's head. Sixteen thousand dollars was twice the largest payroll he had ever handled . . . and that one he had taken by coach with a driver and another man riding shotgun.

'Imagine what you can do with a thousand dollars.' Jim was giving him encouragement. 'You want to start a ranch? How about setting up your own trading post? You could start your own freight operation.' He again showed his teeth in a wide smile. 'Hear what I'm saying? You can do anything you want once the job is done.'

'A man has to be alive to spend money, Jim. This sounds about as risky as swapping bites with a Diamondback Rattlesnake!'

'A three-to-four-day job,' Jim ignored his concern. 'Think of it, Lucas. You can be set for life!'

'Or it'll be the end of my life,' Lucas shot back. 'Sixteen thousand dollars is more than most men will earn in their lifetime. If word gets around — '

'We aren't going to advertise the delivery — not until the job is complete anyway. We might be able to use it as an incentive for other prospective customers later.'

Lucas still didn't like the idea. All that money, plus two unknown men to accompany him, riding through a war zone to a gold mine . . . it was not a job he would have asked anyone else to take.

'You're my last and only hope,' Jim was saying. 'If I have to hire twenty men to do the job, it will end up costing me more than the company will make. Besides which, a war party might think they are coming to fight and ambush them. This is the only thing that makes sense — sneak in three experienced men, make the delivery, and be out of the territory before anyone knows you are there.'

'All right, Jim,' Lucas finally gave in. 'I'll take the job, but it'll be the last one. Once I get paid, I'm looking to start my own ranch or business.'

Jim's face lit up, practically beaming. 'You won't regret it, Lucas,' he said happily. 'Believe me, this is going to be a good deal for both of us!'

'When do I leave?'

★   ★   ★

Daniel walked into the trading post, wearing the garb of a drifter. His long hair was tucked up under a wide-brimmed hat; his cotton shirt was rolled at the sleeves to above his elbows, and the heavy denim pants were over miner's work boots. Being lighter-skinned than most Indians, he often moved about as a regular cowboy or drifter. He could keep tabs on what was going on without raising suspicion.

The girl surprised him, popping up from behind the counter, where she had obviously been doing some cleaning or storing goods on a low shelf. She flashed a professional smile in greeting.

'Hello!' she said. 'Can I help you?'

'I was looking for Tolberg,' Daniel replied. 'Who are you?'

'I'm his niece, Iris Ducane.'

Daniel was about to reach for his hat, to remove it in a polite salutation, but caught himself. It wouldn't do to have his black mane drop down about his shoulders. A good many men wore long hair, but he looked much more Indian with his hair down.

'I'm Daniel Books,' he said, offering

her his best smile. 'I have to say you seem more than a little out of place here at this trading post.'

'So I'm reminded most every day,' she said. 'Uncle Hank is out back, cutting wood for the winter store.'

'I need about five hundred rounds of .44 rimfire cartridges for my Winchester.'

'You figure on starting a war?' the girl teased.

Daniel laughed. 'I'm buying for several other miners and we don't get over to this part of the country very often. We have to stock up when we get the chance. Never know when we might run into trouble.'

She glanced at the ammo shelf. 'We don't have near that many cartridges in stock.'

'No problem, I'll take what you have.'

'It seems there has been a lot of activity since men started going into the Black Hills.' She began to set boxes of cartridges on the counter. 'Just a couple days back, a man brought in a

Cheyenne woman and her child. Her traveling companions had been killed by some renegade Sioux.'

Daniel shook his head. 'There's still a lot of petty fighting going on between the tribes. Some war chiefs haven't come to realize that their real enemy is the white man's army.'

'The man who saved the woman was called Lucas.' She spoke the sentence as if making conversation, but Daniel read her interest at once. He hid his own smile.

'Lucas you say?' He paused to rub his chin thoughtfully. 'Seems I've run into him on occasion. Fairly big man, with eyes of flint and the long face of a hound dog?'

'He has gentle eyes and is rather good-looking.'

Daniel laughed and Iris realized he was teasing her. 'You do know him!' she declared.

'I met him when he was taking Pretty Bird back to her camp,' he explained, confiding part of the truth to her. 'He's a brave and honorable sort, I'll give him that.'

'He saved her from being kidnapped by the Sioux,' she said. 'Then, while he was here at the post, a couple of hunters showed up and wanted to drag her out and kill her for revenge. They blamed her for the death of one of their friends and his family. He talked them out of doing her any harm too.'

'Be a real blessing if all men who hated and wanted to kill one another could be turned loose in a special arena together. They could destroy each other without involving everyone else.'

'That's quite philosophical for a miner.'

Daniel was impressed. 'You talk real good — you proper educated?'

'Not formally. Mom taught me. I can read and cipher numbers, plus my dad had some books to read when I was growing up.' She arched her brows. 'Do you disapprove of a woman having a brain?'

Daniel showed his teeth when he

smiled. 'Not at all, ma'am,' he said quickly. 'I sometimes think women are smarter than men. Which one stays to tend the home and fire while the other is out in the freezing cold or burning sun, hunting or riding herd over cattle? Who teaches the kids to be respectful and proper, while the other is working in the fields or mines to bring home a little money? And who is it who moves to a settlement and makes it into a town?' He patted his chest. 'I'm proud to be a man, but I have a great respect for a good woman.'

The challenge left Iris's expression. 'Do you have yourself a good woman?'

'I'm not in the market for one at present,' he replied. 'Time enough for that once I decide where I'm going to make my mark.'

Iris placed the final box of ammo on the counter. 'One hundred rounds is all we have,' she stated. 'Anything else for you, Mr Books?'

'I don't suppose Lucas said when he'd be back?'

She attempted not to show a special interest. 'He didn't say for certain, but I'm pretty sure he will be coming back.'

'With you here, thinking of him the way you do?' Daniel laughed. 'Yeah, he'll be coming back as quick as his horse will carry him. He might be a little thick under the hat, but he will sure enough want to see you again.'

Iris could not hide the blush, but she smiled all the same. 'You didn't say if there was anything else you needed.'

'That's all for today.'

Iris totaled the amount and he paid her. When he left the trading post, he had to chuckle to himself. Lucas had mentioned the girl, calling her a lively little sprite. After meeting her in person, Daniel had to agree she was something pretty special.

★ ★ ★

The two men were Buck Xylander and Whitey Potts. Buck had the look of a man who belonged on a Wanted poster, rough, unshaven, constantly toying with a well-oiled Colt he carried in a cut-away holster. Whitey was more the talker of the two, but he chewed tobacco and had to pause to spit about every thirty seconds. He wore an Army revolver and carried two rifles — a standard carbine and a Sharps buffalo gun.

Gil Martin was a flashy dresser — expensive suit and hat, polished boots and wearing the smile of a man who had hit the mother lode at his gold mine. He cheerfully signed over a bank note for four thousand dollars and handed a locked strongbox to Lucas.

'The mine foreman has the key,' he said. 'He'll send back a receipt for the box and our business will be complete.'

'I'm sure there will be no problem,' Jim assured the man. 'Lucas here has handled a great number of these deliveries. He's never failed to get the job done.'

'Good, good!' Martin praised. 'I'll be glad to get this matter taken care of.'

'Why so much money all at once?' Jim asked.

'They have a safe at the mine and a twenty-four-hour guard. This should take care of the wages for several months to come. By then I'll have a system set up with the freighting company. They'll bring ore to the smelter and I'll send back a payroll with the empty wagon. As it stands now, I'm behind in paying the men for nearly two months of work. Hate for them to up and quit on account of not being paid.'

'You can consider the delivery the same as done,' Jim boasted. 'Lucas and your two guards should have no trouble.'

'I'll look for you to be back in four to five days,' Martin said, again displaying his million-dollar grin. 'Good luck to you boys.'

Jim also wished them a good trip and Lucas carried the strongbox out to the street and strapped it on behind his saddle. In a matter of minutes, he and the two guards were riding out of town. Whitey took the lead and Buck followed alongside of Lucas.

'Whitey has been there before,' Buck spoke up after they had gone about a mile. 'He knows the main trails too.'

'I've been through the country a time or two myself,' Lucas replied. 'I hadn't heard of anyone hitting a big strike.'

'Martin is keeping mum about it, so as not to have a host of claim jumpers trying to horn in on his dig. Way he tells it, the miners have hit color, but have not yet located the major vein or mother lode. Makes sense to keep it under his hat.'

Those were the last words offered by Buck. They rode until nearly dark, traveling some forty miles, before Whitey left the trail and located a small clearing.

'This ought to do us nicely for the night,' he said. 'Very few people use this lower trail and the Indians prefer to keep to the higher ground so they can watch for army patrols.'

'How far is the mine?' Lucas asked.

'In the morning, we'll take a short-cut over the foothills and pick up the trail used by the wagons,' Whitey replied. 'We should reach the mine by tomorrow afternoon.'

'I suspect we ought to take turns on the watch,' Lucas suggested. 'Most of the war parties don't come this way, but it wouldn't do for a couple renegades or bandits to catch us all napping at the same time.'

'We'll split the shift into three hours each,' Whitey said. 'Do you have a preference for the watch you take?'

'Early or late is the best for a man actually to get any sleep. Want to toss a coin for it?'

'I'll take the middle shift,' Buck spoke up. 'I can't sleep more than a couple hours at a time.'

'Since the war,' Whitey explained. 'Roof fell on us when we were sleeping one night . . . courtesy of a Reb cannon. Buck here has never been much for sleeping indoors or very soundly since that night.'

'You weren't the one buried alive for six hours,' Buck pointed out.

'No, I was opposite the main ceiling beam that came down. Buck was lucky to have survived. He'd have been crushed except for an old pot-belly stove. The beam landed on it first and prevented it from crushing him to death.'

'Sounds pretty scary all right.'

'Like I said, wake me for the second watch . . . if I happen to be asleep.'

After the horses were tended and tethered, the three ate cold beans and hard rolls. Buck and Whitey turned in, while Lucas made a quiet circle of the camp and found himself a scenic spot from which to keep watch.

He had time to think, sitting and watching the darkness come. It would be a couple hours before the moon put in an appearance, so it was dark and quiet . . . other than for a distant owl. It gave a double-hoot every couple minutes, as if trying to coax a bird of the opposite sex to come and join him.

Allowing his mind to wander was a one-way path since meeting the exciting girl at Tolberg's place. Iris was her name, as bright as a ray of sunshine and full of spunk like a month-old colt. He wondered how she was going to behave when he saw her next. With a thousand dollars to his name, he had any number of opportunities. It would be nice to have a wife at his side, and the two of them could decide their future together.

Wonder how long a man should know a woman before he proposes marriage?

Coming back to the present, he reluctantly pushed the girl from his thoughts. He still had a job to do. They would deliver the money box tomorrow and be on their way back to Crossbow the following morning. Until then, he only had to concern himself with his two companions and any trouble they might run into along the way.

Considering the pair of ex-Yanks, they seemed cut out for this sort of job. Both men were hard as rail-road spikes, carried their guns like they knew how to use them and were vigilant of their surroundings. The fact they didn't talk while riding was part of their natural training. A man couldn't stop his horse from snorting or stepping on a dry twig, but the human voice was a dead giveaway. When in Indian country, you rode like they did — quiet, using hand signals and staying low in the brush. You didn't offer a silhouette to an enemy and never strayed in the open when there was any kind of cover nearby.

As his third hour of watching was nearing its end, he heard the soft sound of footsteps. He readied his rifle as Buck suddenly appeared out of the darkness. Considering Lucas had not made a sound, it was a surprise to have the man walk right over to where he was sitting.

'Reckon it's my turn,' Buck said softly. 'Hope Whitey don't start snoring or you won't get a wink of sleep until he has to relieve me.'

'I don't sleep soundly on the trail,' Lucas replied, 'but a few minutes of resting with my eyes closed would be nice.'

'If he starts sounding off like a snorting elk, just flip him a turn on to his stomach. I've rolled that noise-maker over more than once to quiet him.' Buck uttered a grunt. 'It don't even wake him up!'

Lucas chuckled and got to his feet. 'I'll see you in the morning.'

'See ya then,' Buck replied.

5

Daniel hated the idea of a coming war, but it was beyond talk now. The Black Hills of the Dakotas, which had been designated as Indian Territory, had been overrun by gold seekers. The soldiers would come and he was a member of the Cheyenne. Being able to pass for white allowed him to buy ammunition and rifles, but it was a heavy burden on his conscience. He recalled his conversation with Lucas about how the end of the Indian way was inevitable. There would be no stopping the westward movement of the settlers, ranchers and miners. One day they would occupy the land from ocean to ocean.

However, the Indians had gained some advantage for the impending war. They had managed to acquire a significant number of new Winchesters.

The Cavalry would be at a distinct disadvantage with their single-shot carbines. Perhaps the War Department didn't think soldiers needed up-to-date weapons to defeat a bunch of ignorant savages. If so, it would be a costly mistake when the battle started.

Suddenly, there came the sound of two gunshots, fired almost simultaneously. Daniel stopped his horse and listened. He heard distant voices, gruff, as if there was an argument, then only the stillness of the day. After a few seconds, he eased his horse up the trail.

He had gone a short distance when he spotted a horse. It was saddled, without a rider and the reins were dragging on the ground. He didn't know the horse, but he recognized the polished rifle butt sticking from the boot next to the saddle. It was the same one Lucas had been carrying with him when he came to Ghost Bull's camp.

Moving slowly, so as not to spook the horse, Daniel rode over and caught up the reins. Then, with the animal in tow, he turned to follow the prints of the riderless horse. It didn't take long to find the owner.

Lucas was lying face-down at the bottom of a wash. It appeared he had been shot while moving along the back of the ridge, had fallen from his horse and rolled down the hill. Daniel could see no footprints, no tracks of other horses, leading down the steep embankment. Whoever had ambushed Lucas had not bothered to check on his condition.

Daniel rode a short way along the crest until he was able to spy two distant horsemen. They were moving at a rapid pace, already down to the lower foothills. Both men were too far away to make out their features, but it was obvious they were not coming back.

After picking up Lucas's horse, Daniel selected a route down to the bottom of the ravine and turned back up the wash toward Lucas. It took only about five minutes to reach his body. A quick inspection showed a crimson blotch from blood and two bullet holes in the back of his shirt. It was a surprise to discover the man wasn't dead . . . not yet.

★ ★ ★

Iris was hanging out the laundry when she saw the approach of a rider, leading a second horse. It took a moment before she realized there was a body draped over the animal. She left the basket of clothing and hurried into the trading post to call her uncle.

Hank was there to meet the new arrivals. Iris recognized the man who had purchased ammunition from them a short time back. When she saw the unconscious man was none other than Lucas she gasped in shock!

'Dear Lord, no!' she cried. 'It's Mr Lucas!'

'What happened, Daniel?' Hank asked, hurrying around to check the body. 'Is he dead?'

'Not yet . . . or he wasn't when I

loaded him on to his horse,' Daniel answered.

'How and where did you find Mr Lucas?' Iris wanted to know.

'Don't know the whole of the matter,' Daniel answered. 'He was on a trail leading back into the Black Hills. It appears two men dry-gulched him, but from the tracks, it looks as if they were riding together. Lucas must have been out in front, 'cause both shots were in his back.'

'He's still breathing. Let's get him into the bedroom,' Hank directed. 'I haven't had to remove any bullets for some time, but it's not something a man forgets.'

'He don't look good,' Daniel pointed out. 'He would have been killed outright, but he has a whooping big knife strapped to his back. Appears one of the bullets struck the blade and bounced off.'

'Yeah, even as a kid, he always carried a knife like the one Jim Bowie had. He said it had saved his hide a couple of times — never from being shot in the back though.'

'It hasn't saved his life yet,' Daniel said. 'He still has one bullet in him and he hasn't made a peep since I loaded him over his horse.'

'Grab his feet and cut him loose. I've got his shoulders.'

Daniel removed the rope holding Lucas in place and the two men carried him into the trading post.

Iris had her bed ready by the time they got there, quickly stepping aside so they could put him down.

'Face down,' Hank instructed. 'I'll need to do some doctoring right quick.'

Daniel said, 'There's no exit wound, so the bullet is still in there.'

'I've got my old medical kit from when I served in the war,' Hank told him. 'I've had to use it a time or two before.'

'You a for real doctor?' Daniel asked.

'Medico with the Union army for a couple years. Never had any real training — started out carrying stretchers and helping one of the few doctors we had. Next thing I was doing the simple surgeries and such.' He shrugged. 'It was either that or let the men die. One or two doctors couldn't handle a hundred wounded and dying men all at once.'

'What do you need from me?' Daniel asked.

'Iris . . . we'll need some hot water and round up some clean cloth we can use for bandages. Daniel, I'll need you to help me with Lucas. Can't have him coming awake about the time I stick a blade into his back to remove the bullet.'

'He's bled quite a bit.'

'I'll cauterize the wound once I get the bullet out. I don't see any foam and can't hear air escaping so that's good.'

'Meaning it missed the lungs?'

'You got it, son. Get his shirt off while Iris gets the bandage and water. I'm going to grab my medical kit and we'll get started.'

Iris didn't listen further. She hurried to get the hot water. As she had been doing laundry, she had a pot already heating on the stove. The bandage would be whatever had already dried on the clothesline. She would cut it into usable strips.

'Please, God,' she murmured. 'Please don't let Lucas die.'

★   ★   ★

Jim was crestfallen. He sank down behind his desk and placed his head between his hands at the dreaded news.

'They must have seen the strongbox on the back of his horse,' Whitey continued with the story. 'We figure six or seven men in the bunch, too many for us to take on in a gunfight.'

'You're certain Lucas was killed?' Jim asked softly.

'They kilt his horse with the first volley of shots. Buck and me took cover and throwed a few shots, but they gunned down Lucas before he could get free of his mount. I figure they hit him no less than five or six times.'

'Like Whitey says,' Buck joined in. 'We didn't stand a chance against a half-dozen heavily armed men. We had to hightail it or be killed along with Lucas.'

'We didn't get a good look at any of them,' Whitey picked up again. 'All we saw was the smoke from all of their rifles. They peppered us with lead until we were out of range. It's durn lucky neither of us was hit.'

The two men went silent and Jim could not find words. A sob of grief rose in his throat, both for the loss of his friend and the sizable loss of money. The founder and owner of the bank was going to be very unhappy at suffering such a devastating expense. Crossbow had been earning barely enough to break even. With the loss of this payroll, the profits from a couple of the larger banks would have to be used for the reimbursement. Fortunately, he had wired and received approval about the insurance before authorizing the deal. But he had vouched for the trustworthy nature of his hired man, Lucas. He would still be held responsible.

'Am I interrupting?' Gil Martin had entered the room. 'I saw the two hired guards return and figured you had good news for me.'

Jim looked up, as Whitey and Buck backed away from his desk. Neither of them looked at Martin.

'We didn't make it,' Jim told the man. 'My courier and his horse were both killed in an ambush before delivery could be made.'

'We had no chance,' Whitey spoke up to the man. 'It was run or die.'

Martin nearly fell to his knees. 'No!' he gasped, shaking his head back and forth. 'The mine . . . the payroll . . . I'll be ruined.'

'I wouldn't try a trip like that again with less than twenty men,' Whitey said. 'And even then it would be a fight. If we avoided the bandit gang, we could still run into an Indian war party and maybe not make it there either.'

'The ride to your mine won't be safe

until the government sends in troops and cleans out each nest of bandits and every renegade Indian in the country,' Buck added. 'Tell you straight, we ain't going back.'

'Buck's right, that was too close for us,' Whitey joined in. 'We're not making that trip a second time . . . no matter what the pay!'

Martin rolled his eyes and set his teeth, his features flooded with the pain of defeat. 'The miners will quit and I won't even be able to pay all of my creditors. Without the mine producing ore, I'm busted.'

'I'll have a bank draft for you today,' Jim promised. 'As agreed upon, it will be in the amount of sixteen thousand dollars.'

The broken man waved a hand, as if he cared little about the reimbursement. 'Yes, yes, I'll be back in a couple hours to settle up. I . . . I need a drink.'

Jim watched him turn and trudge out of the room. Whitey and Buck still looked like a couple of whipped dogs.

'Reckon we'll take our leave too and head over for a drink or two ourselves,' Whitey said. 'We're damn sorry, Mr Grogan.'

'Lucas seemed a good man,' Buck added. 'Hated like hell to see him gunned down like a rabid dog.'

Jim could not speak, waiting until the two men had left him alone in his office. Once the door closed, Jim ducked his head and blinked against the tears in his eyes. He had talked Lucas into taking the job, used their history together to twist his arm, and it had cost the man his life.

'I'm sorry, Lucas,' he whispered aloud, suffering a heavy burden of regret. He had let his desire for success overrule his better judgment . . . and his friend had paid the price.

* * *

Lucas was borderline sentient, his senses sluggish as he labored to lift his benumbed brain out of a thick, clinging fog. Odd bits of dreams flashed through his head, either mental images he could not distinguish or blurred visions which made no sense. He might have let go of what awareness he could muster if not for the soft murmur that occasionally penetrated his haze.

The words were sweet and melodic, like an angel's whisper, coaxing him to rise above the dark curtain which imprisoned him in a tomb of limbo. He battled to hear the words more clearly and made a concentrated effort to come awake.

'That's it, big boy,' the angel cajoled him. 'Open your eyes and look at me with the same hungry, captivating gaze as before you were shot.'

Lucas blinked and opened his eyes. There came an immediate gasp of surprise. He couldn't focus, his vision impaired by too much sleep and the brightness of the single lamp in the room.

'Good Lord Almighty, Lucas!' the familiar feminine voice exclaimed. 'You scared the be-Jesus out of me!'

He could make her out now; Iris was at his bedside, a folded cloth in her hand. She was staring at him with a curious anxiety, as if uncertain that he was truly there or if he was asleep with his eyes open.

'Thought — ' He had to swallow to gather enough moisture to speak. 'Thought I'd taken that trip to the Great Beyond,' he managed weakly.

Iris hurried to put a cup of water to his lips. He drank several swallows, slaking the arid dryness of his throat. When she pulled the cup away, he attempted a smile.

'Durned if I wasn't right,' he said hoarsely. 'I knew it was an angel speaking to me.'

'If you don't beat all,' she retorted a bit sharply. 'Here you are, one step away from the devil's door, and you're trying to sweet talk me!'

'The devil can wait,' he said. 'I'd rather stick here with you.'

That prompted a soft laugh. 'Lucas,

you are about the most singular gent I ever met.'

'Singular?' he repeated. 'Do that mean not married?'

'Among other things,' she replied. 'Are you ready to quit lying about getting babied?'

'Is that what I've been doing?'

'You've a hole in your back from being shot,' she told him. 'And Uncle Hank didn't do you any favors removing the bullet. I swear he did everything but stomp around in your wound with his dirty boots.'

Lucas eased his shoulders forward gently and was rewarded by a jolt of severe pain. He clenched his teeth to keep from groaning and decided he would not be up to chopping wood in the next day or two.

'How'd I get here?'

'Daniel Books found you. He's been sleeping in the loft out at the barn since he brought you in. He seems genuinely concerned about your condition.'

'Looks like taking Pretty Bird home

was a good idea after all.'

'Yes, he claims he would have left you for the buzzards if you hadn't done the tribe a favor. I have to wonder how a white man knows so much about your dealings with the Indians.'

He didn't elaborate about Daniel. 'How long have I been unconscious, Bright Eyes?'

'Three days . . . counting back from the time Daniel found you.'

'I'd like to speak to him.'

'After you've eaten something,' she said firmly. 'You need to get back your strength. I don't intend to have you sleeping in my bed for several weeks.'

'I feel right special, you giving up your own bed.'

The corners of her mouth lifted in a quirky sort of smile. 'Don't feel too special, big boy,' she quipped. 'We had a dog for a time and he used to sleep there too.'

Lucas smiled at her humor. 'Like I said before, you're a remarkable gal.'

'I'll bring you something to eat and

tell Daniel you're back with the living.'

'Much obliged.'

The girl left the room, but was hardly out the door before Daniel appeared. He grinned, seeing Lucas was conscious and alert.

'I'm kind of disappointed,' he said in greeting Lucas. 'I wanted to be the one sitting at your side and holding your hand when you woke up.'

'You'll pardon me if I prefer the young lady.'

He chuckled. 'No offense taken.'

'You found me?' Lucas was immediately serious. 'What about the other two men I was riding with?'

Daniel frowned. 'You didn't pick the best pair to ride with, my friend. They are the ones who shot you in the back and left you to die. If that giant-sized knife hadn't stopped one of the bullets, you'd be looking at the underside of several feet of dirt right now.'

'Reckon they took the strongbox.' It was not a question.

'Nothing on your horse but a saddle

and your rifle and gear, Lucas. It appears they took you by surprise and left you to die.'

'I let my guard down with them,' he admitted. 'I figured if they were not on the level, they would have tried to pull something during the night when we were camped. When they didn't try anything I began to trust them.'

'I think they waited to get well off of the main trails — didn't want your body being found too soon.'

'Right careless of them to leave me alive,' Lucas said.

'You were knocked from your saddle and rolled down into a gully,' Daniel told him. 'I guess they didn't want to take the time to climb down the steep bank. Lucky for you.'

'Yeah, I feel lucky about now.'

Daniel showed his grin a second time. 'You don't know the half of it — Hank hasn't used his questionable surgical skills to remove anything bigger than a thorn for a decade. He dug around for that bullet like a mole looking for grubs.'

'I do have considerable stiffness between my shoulders, but I'd like to change position.'

'What can I do to help?'

'The young lady is fixing me something to eat,' Lucas explained. 'I don't want to be spoon-fed like a baby. If I can sit up a little, I believe I can manage eating on my own.'

Daniel gathered a couple thick blankets and folded them for a back support. As Lucas was lying on the bed with his head nearest the wall, he gently lifted him forward and placed the padding behind his back and shoulders. When finished, Lucas eased gingerly against the makeshift support.

'Ah-h-h,' he said, after the pain subsided to a dull throbbing, 'That's better.'

'You have a little color today,' Daniel said. 'When I brought you in, we didn't have much hope you'd make it. I don't imagine being tied over your horse did much to help your condition.'

'How'd you happen to find me?'

'I was on the upper trail when I heard the shots. By the time I came down the hogback ridge and spied you at the bottom of a wash, those other two fellows were a half-mile away and riding hard.'

Lucas eyed his savior critically. 'And where were you headed . . . dressed like a white man?'

Daniel forced a smile. 'Noticed I had changed out of my buckskins, huh?' He shrugged. 'I was on my way to Henderson's trading post to buy a few things.'

'Henderson has a pretty good store of rifles and ammo at his place. From what I've heard, he'll deal with about anyone.'

Daniel tried to laugh off his remark. 'I could take that as an accusation, Lucas.'

'A man who tries to ride both sides of the fence usually ends up with a sore backside, my good friend.'

'What do you mean, Lucas?'

'You're buying guns and ammunition for the upcoming war.'

The guilt on Daniel's face told him it was the truth, but he tried to deny it. 'I don't know what you're talking about.'

'I've stopped in at most of trading posts in this part of the country and I've heard of a man who is buying up enough ammo and guns for a war. I can understand you wanting to help the Indians, Daniel, but you'll be hanged if you're caught.'

'So what if the Indians have better weapons than the soldiers — it will make no difference in the long run.'

'You admit a few repeating rifles are not going to change the outcome, Daniel. So why risk being caught?'

'I've lived with those people for the last dozen years. I'm related to several of Ghost Bull's family.'

'Yes, but you lived with a white man for the first half of your life.'

'Winning a battle or two might force the government to reconsider the war. They might offer a larger reservation or other concessions to stop the fighting.'

'Your efforts will only get more men killed.'

'I don't see it that way,' Daniel argued. 'I'm giving the Indians a fighting chance.'

'They have no chance!' Lucas fired back at him. 'The tribes could muster every warrior within a thousand miles and they would still have no chance of winning in a war against the government troops. The only thing a small victory will do is give them false hope. They will fight longer and more will die because of that hope.'

'You can't be sure of that.'

'How many warriors have gathered for this war?'

'I don't know, maybe fifteen or twenty thousand.'

'Over half a million men died in the war between the Union and the Confederacy, Daniel, and that was with men fighting against their neighbors and brothers. The army will send however many men it takes to win this war and they won't stop until all resistance is gone.'

'What can I do, Lucas?' Daniel asked. 'I don't belong with either side. I'm a man without a country.'

'All the more reason not to fight on one side or the other.'

'Yeah? Well, what should I be doing?' he asked. 'What can I do to earn a living if I leave the tribe? Most people won't hire a half-Indian.'

'You can work with me.'

'You?' he scoffed at the idea. 'Doing what?'

'I need a partner,' Lucas told him. 'I'm going to find the two men who ambushed me.'

'And why would I want to help you?'

'I can think of eight hundred reasons — each of those reasons being worth a dollar.'

Daniel's eyes opened wider. 'You got that much money stashed away?'

'The bank will pay a recovery fee of ten per cent on what was stolen. We only have to catch those two men and get the money back.'

'Oh, that's all,' he jeered. 'You're maybe forgetting that they will have a couple weeks head-start and will have found a nice burrow to hide in by this time.'

'They think I'm dead,' Lucas said. 'I'm betting they went to the bank with a story about us being ambushed. No one suspects them of anything; they are free to start over wherever they want.'

That news caused Daniel to think. 'What if they've spent some of the money?'

'We'll take the two back-shooters to the law in Crossbow with whatever they have left. Every dollar earns a dime. Its honest money and the only fight you have to join is the one between those two men and me.' Lucas made a face. 'Of course, you have to stay my partner — no changing sides if they make you a better offer.'

'I knew there would be a catch,' Daniel joked.

'What do you say?'

Daniel stuck out his hand. 'All right, I'm not keen on watching men die on either side of the upcoming Indian war. If you really want me to ride along with you, I'll give it a go. What's our first move?'

6

Iris was getting water from the nearby creek when she spied Daniel saddling his horse. She carried the two full buckets of water to the corral and set them down.

'Are you leaving us?' she asked him.

Daniel smiled at her, while tightening the cinch on his horse. 'You are on your own with Lucas, Miss Iris. I've got an errand to run.'

She frowned. 'Uncle Hank says you are buying ammunition for the Indians. If war comes, you could be hanged for it.'

'Your injured pal gave me the same warning — made me an offer to get out of the gun-running business,' Daniel updated her. 'I'm not a fool. I know that in a war with the whites the Indian people are going to lose. I was trying to do something noble, helping my blood kin, but Lucas made me see how it would only make things worse.'

His words caused her stern look to dissipate. 'I'm glad you are going to quit before you get caught. You have shown yourself to be a man with a good heart and I would hate to see you hanging from the end of a rope.'

'Not a thought I want going through my head when I lie down to sleep at night either,' he admitted.

'So this errand, it has nothing to do with the Indians?' At the negative bob of his head, she said, 'Then is it connected to Lucas being shot?'

'You're on the nosey side, aren't you?'

She gave him a smug look. 'I like to be informed of what's going on . . . especially when it involves a man who is recovering in my bed.'

Daniel laughed. 'Best watch how you word that when other people are around. You could get yourself a bad reputation real quick.'

Instead of replying to his barb, she

stayed on the original subject. 'You're doing something for Lucas, aren't you?'

'Did I say you were nosey?' He grunted, 'You're downright meddlesome.'

'Is Lucas going after the men who shot him?'

'You have to ask?' Daniel said, taking a moment to tie his bedroll behind the saddle with the two rawhide straps. 'Man like him, double-crossed, shot and left for dead, and his friend losing a pile of money? Yeah, he's going to find them — we're going to find them.'

'I'm glad he will have help,' she said. 'You seem capable and I think you are trustworthy too.'

'Stop,' he said, 'you'll be causing my head to swell with all of your flattery.'

Iris stooped over and picked up the two buckets of water again. 'Be careful, Daniel,' she said in a serious tone of voice. 'I wouldn't want to see you get hurt.'

'You take care of Lucas,' Daniel told her. 'I'll be back in a week — maybe less — and I expect him to be able to sit his horse and be ready to ride.'

'He'll be ready when he's recovered fully,' she said stubbornly, 'so you needn't hurry your trip.'

He laughed and mounted the horse. 'At least I know he's getting the best of care.' He neck-reined the horse to the trail and waved. 'See you on my return, little wildcat.'

Iris couldn't wave without putting down the buckets, but she did reward him with a smile. By the time she reached the front door, he was lost to the distant trees.

'Only be three of us for supper,' Hank told her, as she carried the water toward the kitchen area. 'Daniel is leaving us for a spell.'

Iris stopped, set down the buckets and looked back at him. 'Yes, he said he's doing some chore for Lucas.'

'That's good. I'm glad to hear he isn't going to be buying guns and ammunition for the Indians any more.' He shrugged his bony shoulders. 'I come close to turning him in a time or two, but he is half-Cheyenne. It makes it hard to call a man a traitor if he is living with and related to the enemy.'

'I agree.'

Hank wrinkled his nose. 'What's that there smell?' he asked, leaning over to take a whiff of her hair. 'You been rubbing up against some wild rose or something?'

'It's called perfume,' she told him pointedly, 'and it's the only bottle we had on the shelf. It must be twenty years old.'

He cackled like an old hen. 'You done got it bad, don't you?'

'What?' she asked.

'I thought you were looking to slip a ring through the captain's nose or pick out a man of wealth for your husband? Lucas didn't get a dime for the payroll delivery, 'cause he never finished the job. He's worth a good horse and a few dollars, that's it.'

'You're the one who told him about the job,' she reminded her uncle. 'You about got him killed, just so he could earn some big money. If that's what it costs to be rich, I'll settle for someone a little on the poorer side.'

Hank gave her a closer look. 'Why are you so taken with him? You only met him the one time and he's been unconscious until today.'

'A favorite uncle of mine once told me how the heart seems to have a mind of its own — do you remember that little chat?'

'Man opens his mouth too often around a woman, he's bound to say something stupid,' he made an excuse. 'You done played on my affection for you and got me talking nonsense.'

'You were telling me about a woman named Lola who sang like an angel.'

'I tell you where to store the sorghum ten times before you get it right, but I mention one single thing about some gal from a lifetime ago and you remember every word!'

She laughed. 'A woman has a convenient recollection, Uncle. We take special care to recall every detail of things we are interested in and discard anything that might cloud our memory.'

'Yeah, your ma was like that when we was growing up. I lost track of how many times I showed her how to skin a rabbit or clean a fish for cooking. Seems I ended up with every dirty chore she didn't like . . . 'cause she couldn't remember or get the hang of how to do it.'

'Being physically weaker than a man, a woman uses what I call feminine manipulation to get what she wants.'

'That's sure enough the two-dollar term for it. We men call it being ornery or stubborn.'

She smiled and asked, 'Would you bring in some more wood for the stove? I have to get some of this water heating.'

'We got another term for when you females ask us to do something in a manner that don't allow for us to say no — it's called being henpecked!'

Iris had taken Lucas his breakfast and chatted with him while he ate. It took most of his strength to feed himself, but he refused to let her wait on him. Once finished, he seemed to drift off to sleep in the middle of her talking about growing up on a farm.

For a short time she remained watching over him, half afraid he would suddenly become worse — struck by fever or infection — and perhaps die. She spoke softly to him, words of encouragement and support . . . until he managed a half-smile and murmured an audible, '*Thanks, Bright Eyes.*'

She was returning with the empty plate and cup when a familiar form filled the front door. Her heart sank at seeing Captain Philippe Bagot stride into the trading post.

'*Bonjour*, Mademoiselle Ducane,' Philippe greeted her. 'Is it not appropriate that your name stands for rainbow and also a flower? For truly, you are as sweet as a flower and as breathtaking as a rainbow.'

'Philippe,' she returned a cordial welcome, 'what brings you here today?'

He appeared taken back by her question. 'I told you I was due some time off. It seems we may be at war very soon, so I chose to take leave before we are called to action.'

'War?'

'The numerous tribes have been gathering for some time, making talk and plans for war. We have a great number of troops headed this way. I believe there will be a great battle very soon.'

'How dreadful.'

'Yes, we should do our picnic or riding close to the main roads. It is not safe back in the hills at this time.'

She turned for the kitchen counter, where she had water in a large pan for washing the dishes before drying and putting them away. Philippe followed along wordlessly, but took notice that the table had not yet been cleared.

'You have company?' he asked. 'I see there are two settings at the table and you have a third in your hands.'

'Mr Lucas was shot and left for dead,' she told him. 'Daniel Books found him and brought him to us. Uncle Hank dug out the bullet, but Mr Lucas very nearly died.'

His mood darkened. 'I know of this man, Daniel. I believe he has been buying guns and ammunition for the Indians. He is a traitor.'

She laughed at the absurdity of the accusation. 'If Daniel is working for the Indians, why would he save the life of Mr Lucas?'

'Perhaps Mr Lucas is also in league with the savages.'

'Mr Lucas was taking a payroll to one of the mines. He was ambushed by the two men who were supposed to be helping to guard the delivery.'

'How do you know this?'

'Mr Lucas came to long enough to explain about the payroll. And Daniel saw the two men ride away after they shot Lucas in the back and left him for dead.'

'So you only have the word of a rascal who deals with the Indians?'

Iris was suddenly annoyed with Philippe. He had seemed interesting and exciting, with an ease of conversation and a smooth line of flattery. But questioning her about Lucas and Daniel, accusing them of dealing guns and ammunition to the Indians — regardless of the fact Daniel had been doing exactly that — caused her to become defensive. And it was not hard to defend Daniel, because he was a member of the Cheyenne tribe. He had only been trying to help his people.

'I can't go riding or on a picnic with you, Philippe,' she said, returning to his purpose for the visit. 'We have a number of fresh hides to be treated today and I have a severely injured man to care for.'

'The hides can wait and your uncle can watch over Lucas,' he said callously. 'He would have done the same thing before you came here to join him. You are young and beautiful; you should not be bound to this dusty old shanty.'

'Dusty?' Her temper flared. 'I spend half of every day sweeping and cleaning! I'll bet this trading post is cleaner than your officer's quarters!'

'Forgive me, *s'il vous plait*,' he pleaded. 'I did not intend an insult. I merely wanted you to realize that there is a life beyond these walls.'

'I'm sorry, but I can't leave my work or my patient.'

Philippe momentarily ceased his polite persuasion, growing impatient. 'I think you are infatuated with Monsieur Lucas, my little flower. You refuse to leave his side because it is exactly where you wish to be!'

'Think what you like, Philippe,' she replied sharply. 'I'm not going to leave my uncle alone, not with a wounded man to tend to, and you are making me angry with your childish accusations. I thought you were a gentleman, but I see you can be petty and jealous too.'

The words smarted and Philippe immediately regained his composure. 'I apologize if I have upset you, my dear. I have a duty to perform as an officer, but I should strive to confine my visit to the reason I am here. I wish only to court you properly.'

'I've told you that the seriousness of Lucas's injuries will not allow me to leave him at this time. If you were the one lying in bed, after having a bullet removed from within an inch of your heart, I doubt you would want me to go off to a picnic with someone else.'

'*Oui*, I understand.'

'I'm sorry you made the trip for nothing, Philippe.'

The man summoned his poise and a smile magically appeared. 'It is never a waste of time coming to see you, my little flower. I will not say goodbye, but *à tout à l'heure* — see you later.'

'Yes, until another time,' Iris replied politely. Then she returned to clearing the dishes from the table. Philippe rotated about and walked away, erect as a statue, leaving the room with his conceit intact.

If pride were brains, she thought to herself, *Philippe would be the smartest man alive.*

★ ★ ★

Lucas was able to dress himself on the fourth morning. By the time Iris came to check on him, he had his boots on and had risen to his feet.

'What do you think you're doing?' she complained in a strong tone of voice. 'You've only been in bed a couple of days. You're not ready to be up and around!'

'Can't heal a wound by lying on a bed and being waited on . . . no matter how pretty the nurse. If I become too weak or too pampered, I'll never want to get up again.'

She eyed him with a peculiar sort of interest. 'You called me pretty?'

'Like an evening sunset,' a grin came to his face, 'with about the same amount of dazzling radiance and fire.'

His words caused her to smile as well. 'How long did it take you to conjure up that bit of flattery?'

'I'm been lying here for the past few days with nothing else to do.'

'Is there anything else you'd like to tell me, perhaps some other flattery you've memorized?'

'Took all of my courage to get that much said.'

The smile faded and she put a hard look on him. 'Then take those boots off and get back to bed!'

'Just because I don't have any more sweet-talk thought up?'

'No! Because you are not ready to be traipsing around yet. Uncle Hank dug that bullet out like he was using a shovel to spade a garden. You go moving around and you'll start the wound to bleeding. I don't intend to destroy any more of my linen, cutting it into bandage strips, just because you are too bullheaded to take it easy.'

Lucas remained standing and regarded

the girl with a look of amusement. 'Like I said, as much fire as a glowing sunset.'

Iris stepped over next to him, hands on her hips and her slight frame only inches away. 'You saw what I did to those two trappers,' she warned. 'Don't think I won't kick and scratch and bite you too.'

Lucas started to turn and nearly folded down to his knees. Iris jumped forward to get under his arm and help support his weight.

'I told you . . . ' She began.

Lucas reached out, cupped the back of her head in his hand, then leaned down and planted a kiss on her lips.

Iris allowed him to linger for a glorious moment . . . before she reacted! Jerking away from him, she spun from his grasp and stomped down on his foot — hard!

'Yeow!' he wailed, forced to take a backward step and sit down on the bed. He sucked in his breath from the sudden movement, placing a hand to his chest to battle the intense pain.

'I warned you,' Iris said sternly,

although she knelt down in front of him, watching intently, as if prepared to catch him if he collapsed.

Lucas fought down the swells of agony and managed to draw in a couple shallow breaths. After a few moments, he put his stinging foot up across his knee and began to massage the bruised toes through the boot leather. 'You've got more spunk than an unbroken mustang!' he complained. 'Stomp down about as hard too.'

'I never gave you permission to kiss me,' she told him in a matter-of-fact tone of voice. 'I'm not one of your Indian concubines!'

'I don't have any Indian concubines, Bright Eyes,' he responded. 'And I was only trying to show you I'm able to get around on my own.'

'Yes,' she spoke haughtily, 'I see how capable you are . . . of molesting a woman!'

'All right, it was a weak moment,' he pleaded his defense. 'I was out of my head. I didn't know what I was doing.'

'Hah!' she shot back. 'You don't believe I'm dumb enough to fall for an excuse like that, do you?'

He grinned. 'Maybe I was only trying to show you my gratitude?'

'Gratitude is you *thanking* me, big boy,' she said. 'To kiss me is a reward you haven't earned yet.'

'Might you want to share the information about how I earn something like that?'

'First rule — be a gentleman.'

'And the second rule?'

'Let's stick to the first one for now,' she said. 'I'll let you know when we can start with the others.'

'Others?' he made a face. 'How many other rules are there?'

'Too many to count . . . and it's a girl's prerogative to add more any time she wishes.'

'Good thing I stole a kiss,' he grumbled. 'I don't see any way it's ever going to happen again.'

'That's one of the rules.' At his perplexed expression, she showed a pixie simper, 'A young lady can bypass the rules if she chooses to do so.'

Lucas returned to a standing position, although he took a moment to test whether or not he could put weight on his freshly injured foot. 'I'll be checking on my horse now,' he told her. 'I promise not to do anything too strenuous.'

Rather than argue, Iris advised him, 'Breakfast will be ready in a few minutes. As you are full of such vinegar this morning, I'll expect you to eat with Uncle and me at the table.'

'I'm obliged to you and Hank for taking me in,' he told her seriously. 'I'll be sleeping in the barn tonight.'

'Yes, you will,' she agreed. 'If you've the strength to start getting frisky with me, you darn well are ready to give me back my bed.'

He laughed and — surprisingly — Iris laughed as well.

7

Daniel introduced himself to Jim Grogan and relayed what had taken place. When he finished telling him about Lucas, the man exploded.

'I can't believe it!' he shouted. 'Those two hired men shot Lucas in the back and stole the money? Are you sure of this?'

'I was not more than a quarter-mile away when I heard two shots fired at almost the same time. I reached a place where I could see the ridge not more than a minute or two later. I saw those two men pounding leather, heading away from the ridge, and Lucas was lying at the bottom of the wash. There was no one else around.'

'I'm amazed he survived the attack. How is that possible?'

'You know about the big knife he carries?'

'Oh, yeah, like the one Jim Bowie made famous.'

'That's the one — weighs about a pound and has a blade almost as wide as your hand.' Daniel continued. 'One of the bullets bounced off the blade, but the second narrowly missed his heart and lungs. Hank Tolberg was able to dig it out without killing him.'

'So those two filthy back-shooters bushwhacked Lucas and robbed the payroll.' Jim swore softly. 'I lost a pile of money for my bank and Gil Martin left here a broken man. He lost his investment and the mine. He confided to me he had borrowed money from a couple investors and it was going to take every cent of the insurance money to pay them off.'

'His misfortune is not as serious as being shot in the back,' Daniel said. 'I'm interested in what you might know about the two men who were hired — Buck Xylander and Whitey Potts.'

'They claimed to hail from over around Denver — supposed to be well known as hunters and trackers. I believe one or both served for a time scouting for the army, but that's the story they gave Martin. Personally, I had no previous information about either of them.'

'Sounds like they used Martin as a sucker.'

'He took their bait whole,' Jim agreed, 'Me too, for that matter. Both fellows seemed on the level, talking up what they would do with their payment of five hundred each.'

'Do you remember what they said about how they were going to spend their money?'

'The usual stuff, you know — drink, women and merriment, along with possibly starting up a trading post or something of their own. I didn't pay much attention to them or their conversations.'

'You didn't happen to notice which way they went when they left town?'

'No, but the man at the livery might have an idea. One of them mentioned getting new shoes for his horse before they pulled out. Buck, I believe it was, said his mount threw a shoe during their escape.'

Daniel considered how that might help, thinking a horse with new iron would make the two easier to follow. Of course, he still had to find them first.

'Lucas claimed you would pay a reward of ten percent for any money returned.'

'I personally guarantee it,' Jim said, displaying some enthusiasm. 'If you and he can bring back the whole amount, I'll make it a thousand each for the reward.'

'Lucas explained how this insurance thing worked,' Daniel told Jim. 'You had Martin fork over four thousand dollars to cover a payroll of sixteen thousand.'

'That's right. Twenty-five per cent up front.'

'So your loss here at the bank was twelve thousand, is that right?'

'Yes.'

Daniel smiled. 'Then you're mostly interested in getting your money back — the twelve thousand?'

Jim laughed — the first time for him since the robbery. 'I see where this is going. You want to keep anything over the twelve thousand.'

'With a guarantee of at least five hundred each, no matter how much we recover.'

Jim considered his offer. 'I'll go along with that,' then he added to the deal, '*If* you two manage to haul those two men in for trial.'

Daniel stuck out his hand. 'Lucas said you were a good man.'

Shaking his hand, Jim replied, 'We have us a deal.'

'Would you mind walking over to see the livery man with me?' Daniel asked. 'I don't know anyone in town and he might be a little quicker to come forward with the truth if you were there.'

'I'll get my hat,' Jim said. 'If he doesn't wish to tell us what he knows,

I'll have the town marshal speak to him.'

'Much obliged.'

'I'm the one who is obliged,' Jim replied, 'And it's obvious Lucas found the right man to help him find those two bushwhackers.'

'Let's go see what we can find out.'

★　★　★

In an effort to help pay for his keep, Lucas made trips to the surrounding woods and picked up dried branches or hauled dead trees back for cutting into firewood. He had finished one such trip when several riders appeared on the trail. He recognized the uniforms as cavalry and stood back to watch as they arrived.

The lead rider was all too familiar — smart-looking, clean-shaven except for a thin moustache, with a sword on his hip. His chin had a confident lift and he rode with his shoulders erect — the man oozed superiority. Captain

Bagot lifted a hand and called the small group to a halt. Giving the order for the men to dismount and rest their horses, he climbed down and handed the reins of his horse to the man nearest him. He appeared intent upon entering the trading post, but then spied Lucas looking their way. He changed direction and strode over to stop a few feet away.

'You are up on your feet, Monsieur Lucas,' he stated the obvious.

'Hard to keep me down for more than a day or two,' Lucas answered, choosing to ignore the man's use of French in his address.

'You have improved greatly since I last visited. Madamoiselle Iris told me how you had a narrow escape from death.'

'I reckon I was at the crossroads betwixt heaven and hell for a short time,' Lucas replied. 'But I'm getting my strength back.'

'It has been convenient for you having a personal nurse, has it not?'

'Better treatment than a man would

get from one of your army infirmaries,' Lucas said, recognizing a measure of jealousy in Bagot's statement. 'The lady is a good cook and I'd wager a lot better-looking than most of your medical staff too.'

'How long before you leave?' Philippe asked, perceptibly interested.

'Another coupla days.'

Bagot could not hide his surprise. 'That soon? You either were not as badly hurt as I was told or you must heal very quickly.'

'I don't want the trail to get too cold,' Lucas said, without tackling his comment. 'I intend to track down the two men who double-crossed and bushwhacked me.'

'On that endeavor, I wish you luck.'

'Do you and your patrols ever get up into the mining country?'

'On occasion,' Philippe answered. 'There have been a number of gold seekers entering the Black Hills, but many of the prospectors are afraid of Indian reprisals and are waiting for us to deal with the problem.'

'The guy I was transporting the payroll for was named Martin,' Lucas said. 'Don't suppose you know anything about his mine? He said he had about twenty men digging for him, along with a couple of ore wagons.'

'Sounds like a sizable excavation,' Bagot said. 'I have not come across any mining operations of that size. Why do you ask?'

'Martin claimed he would go broke if the miners didn't get paid. I was wondering if they all quit on him.'

'I'm afraid I have no information of interest to pass along.'

'All right, thanks anyway.'

The captain eyed him for a long moment, as if trying to determine something in his own head. Finally, he seemed to have satisfied his curiosity.

'The lady is spoken for — did she tell you?'

'I never asked,' Lucas was nonchalant. 'I imagine she would have mentioned it if the subject had come up.'

'She was quick to take your side concerning the Indian woman you rescued.'

'The woman had a baby, Captain. When it comes to choosing sides, most any gal will defend a mother and child.'

Bagot smiled — less than sincere, but not exactly a smirk. 'You play politics with me,' he said. 'I think you have the mistaken idea that you might stand a chance to win favor with the *mademoiselle*.'

'A man shouldn't try to skin a deer before he's made the shot, Captain. From what little I've learned about Hank's niece, she can be very determined.'

'Even a headstrong woman can be dominated by the right man.'

Lucas gave his head a negative shake. 'If I was you, I wouldn't be too quick to try to *dominate* Miss Ducane. We've agreed she has a will of her own.'

The captain uttered a begrudging chuckle. 'Yes, perhaps I should say a man might be able to manipulate her carefully into doing what he wanted.'

'Providing she has no objection to start with.'

'You are an insightful man, Lucas. I shall remember not to underestimate you in the future.'

Lucas grinned. 'I reckon that's almost a compliment, so I'll just add that I won't underestimate you either.'

Bagot whirled about and headed for the main building. He had obviously stopped by to see Iris . . . but had paused to confront Lucas and try to mark his territory. The captain claimed Iris to be his property, but Lucas had looked into the young woman's eyes. He had seen no measure of ownership by another man. She had behaved like a free spirit ever since he had first met her. Perhaps she had encouraged Bagot, or it might be the man's own arrogance caused him to believe no woman could deny his charm. Whatever the case, Lucas was not going to give the man free rein. If Iris decided to tell him to his face that she was in love with the captain, it would end his pursuit. Until such time, it was every man-jack for himself and may the best man win!

★　★　★

Lucas was able to move about without much pain by the time Daniel returned. It had been ten days since he was shot, and the healing was nearly complete. The only pain was when he moved too quickly or stretched out a little too far with his left arm. It told him the internal healing was taking a bit longer than the external process.

'Our two boys told some guys at the saloon they were going south-east to Denver, but Grogan and I talked to the hostler and he said they left by way of the north end of town heading in the direction of Cheyenne.'

'Did you get to speak to Martin?'

'No, he went back to Denver to return the money his investors had given him. He told Grogan that, after a deadly ambush and losing the payroll, no one would be willing to risk taking so much money into the Dakotas again. Besides which, he had used his own money to purchase the insurance. Without it, he couldn't afford to hire several new men to try again.'

'So the mine closes and all of the miners quit?'

'Far as anyone knows — no pay, no work.'

'Poor guy lost his stake,' Lucas said. 'Wonder what he'll do now?'

'Your pal didn't know that he had any plan except to return the money to the investors.'

'Yes, and the mine probably closed down when no payroll arrived.'

'That's likely.'

'I should have waited until I could meet the ore wagons and made the trip back with them. It would have taken a sizable number of bandits to try and rob me, had I been with several teamsters.'

'Not your fault,' Daniel reasoned. 'The man said the money had to get up there quick to prevent the miners from leaving. He took a chance and lost.'

'Well, we are going to see if we can recover some of the money. Doubt it will help Martin — except on the outside chance we could get back every cent — but it will put Jim back on the good side of his banking partners.'

'So when do we leave?'

'It's going to be dark in a couple hours. We might as well start in the morning.'

'Guess that means I get to share the barn loft with you.'

'Only if you don't start to snore.'

'Indians don't snore,' Daniel pointed out with an air of pomposity. 'It would leave us vulnerable to an attack by giving away our position.'

'Yeah, well if the white half starts to snore, the red half is getting tossed out of the loft at the same time.'

'Damn, you're a touchy sort when it comes to getting your sleep, aren't you?'

★ ★ ★

Lucas allowed Daniel to do much of the saddling and packing of the horses. They were ready to leave shortly after daylight. As Lucas filled his canteen, Hank and Iris came over to see them off.

'Can't say it hasn't been good having you around,' Hank teased. 'Been kind of nice not having to entertain Iris every day by myself.'

'You sure enough saved my life, Hank,' Lucas told him. 'I'll never be able to pay you back for that.'

'Proved to me you are about as tough as a nickel steak, surviving my cutting and prodding for that there bullet.'

'I'm beholden to you all the same.'

Hank lifted a hand and then returned to the trading post. With Daniel fiddling with his own gear, it allowed Iris and Lucas a moment alone.

'I asked Uncle what your full name was, but he said he didn't know you by anything other than just Lucas,' the girl said. 'I think — having allowed you to kiss me and all — I ought to know your whole name.'

Lucas summoned forth a perplexed look and rubbed his freshly shaved chin. 'You allowed me to kiss you? That isn't exactly the way I remember it.'

'You were wounded and could hardly stand up,' she informed him. 'Had I wished to stop you, I would have punched you in the chest. Being injured like you were, it would have knocked you flat.'

The admission caused Lucas to smile. 'Now I begin to see why I've got to come back here when I've finished this little chore.'

'Oh?' Her eyes flashed with impish anticipation. 'You think you might fare as well a second time?'

'For a chance to hold you in my arms, I'd come back from the dead.'

'You still haven't told me your full name,' she countered. 'I'm not making any plans concerning a man with only one name.'

Lucas glanced over to see Daniel was out of earshot. 'If I tell you, it has to stay between us. You can't repeat it to anyone.'

'Don't tell me you are related to some infamous killer or something?' She said. 'Are you a descendant of Benedict Arnold or related to the dastardly Confederate known as Quantrill?'

'I reckon you know many people pass along the surname of their mother's family to the firstborn son. That's what happened in my case.'

'Your mother's last name was Lucas?'

He took a deep breath. 'No, her maiden name was' — again he glanced about nervously — 'Suzanna Darling.'

Iris held an impassive expression . . . for about three seconds, before she burst into a fit of laughter.

Lucas groaned over her lack of control. It only made her enjoy the mirth all the more. When she finally regained some decorum, he shrugged.

'Yeah, well, you can see why the name isn't something I would like bantered about.'

'So your name is Darling Lucas?' she asked.

'Mom wanted to pass along her last

name and she was hoping I would be born a girl. When that didn't pan out, she still decided to use her family name. Dad was working on the railroad and never saw me until I was a year old. By that time, it was too late to change the name, so he simply called me Little Luke.'

'So if a woman calls you *Darling*, it isn't necessarily a term of endearment.'

Lucas smiled. 'Considering you're the only woman who knows the name, Bright Eyes, I would definitely consider it a term of endearment.'

A playful smile played upon Iris's lips. 'Then I think I'd better stick to calling you Lucas.'

He took a step in her direction. 'For one little goodbye kiss, you can call me whatever you like.'

But Iris quickly sidestepped his advance. 'You come back in one piece and then we'll see if this relationship is going to go anywhere, big boy.'

Daniel had mounted and moved up to where they were talking. 'You about ready to get started?' he asked Lucas.

'Reckon so, partner,' he replied. 'The lady here says I have to finish this job before I can come courting.'

Daniel gave a worried bob of his head. 'A prize like her — you best hope we get this sorted out right sudden. I know of a couple young bucks who think she'd make a fine wife, Indian or not.'

Lucas grinned at the remark and, once aboard his horse, he snickered, 'I think, if one of those braves acted on the notion, he would find he had a bull by the tail.'

'Or a wildcat,' Daniel agreed with a smirk of his own.

'You two witty guys better get started, before you lose daylight!' Iris snapped, feigning insult. 'Either that or I lose my temper.'

Lucas and Daniel both laughed and they started off down the trail. When he glanced back, he felt a warm glow. Iris had remained standing in the yard watching. Seeing him looking back, she raised a hand to wave.

Yep, gotta get this settled so I can ride back this way, he decided. *No doubt about it.*

★ ★ ★

They rode until dusk, then camped back in a hollow, which was at the foot of a rocky escarpment. There were enough trees and brush to hide them from the nearest trail and they used dried bark for a smokeless fire.

'I caught up with the latest news when I was in Crossbow,' Daniel spoke, after they had doused the fire and stretched out on their ground blankets. 'A general named Alfred Terry is supposed to be leading a large force of soldiers toward the Dakotas. One report said he and several other generals are supposed to meet somewhere near the Black Hills. They will have several thousand troops between them.' The man uttered a sigh of regret. 'It appears as if the final war is about to begin.'

'Are the Indians prepared to fight against such overwhelming numbers?'

Daniel stared at the night sky, as if he hadn't heard . . . but answered a few moments later. 'There is a mix of tribes readying for war such as I have never seen. The war council is led by several chiefs — Crazy Horse of the Oglalas, Rain-in-face from the Hunkpapa . . . also Low Dog. There is another — Sitting Bull — who sounds like a man of both wisdom and influence. All together there are many bands of Sioux, Cheyenne, some Arapaho and a great many other tribes with a smaller number of warriors. Never have so many come together in one place.'

'And Ghost Bull?'

'He will probably ride with Dull Knife.'

'I fear the wayward life of the nomad Indian is at an end, Daniel. The choice will be to live on a reservation or die in battle.'

'Not a great choice.'

'You don't have to make that decision,' Lucas told him. 'You are half-white and can ride away and start your own life.'

'Let's hope we recover enough money for that to be an option,' Daniel said. 'What about you, Lucas? Have you planned anything beyond trying to win over Hank's niece?'

'I'm thinking of starting a horse ranch — not riding stock, but draft horses and mules for pulling freight wagons and coaches. Plus, once the threat of war is gone, there will be farmers coming to this part of the country by the thousands. There will be a need for plow horses to work the fields too.'

'And what about your girl?'

'That won't be easy,' Lucas admitted. 'I'm not the only one trying to court the young lady, and one of them is a captain stationed over at the fort.'

'I'm not an expert on female folk, but Iris definitely seems to have an interest in you.'

Lucas sighed. 'I hope so, but I worry

she won't wait very long. Not much of a life living with her uncle at that old trading post.'

Daniel grinned. 'Then we'll make short work of this chore, my friend. We only need to catch those two thieves and recover enough money to earn ourselves a fat bonus. She ought to wait long enough for that.'

'I hope you're right, Daniel, I sure do.'

8

They had ridden a few hours the next day when Daniel suddenly stopped his horse. He studied the trail, looked at a slight scrape on the side of a nearby tree and motioned to Lucas.

'Indian sign,' he said in a hushed voice.

'What sign, the tracks from the horses on the trail?'

'No, on the side of the tree,' Daniel said. 'A mark like that allows a scouting party to know the direction the others went whenever they split up. One group is ahead and another moved from the main trail.'

'Scouting parties, headed for Cheyenne?'

'The town is still a long way off. I believe these are my people.'

'You going to bet our lives on that?'

Daniel laughed. 'Follow me, white

man.' And he led the way in the direction of the scouting party.

They came upon them after a short ride — three braves, with bows drawn and arrows ready to fire.

Daniel spoke up to them in their native tongue and called one by name. The three relaxed at once and one came forward to meet with them. He and Daniel conversed for a short time and then Daniel lifted a hand in parting.

'So what's going on?' Lucas asked, as soon as they were headed back to the main trail.

'Something odd,' he answered. 'Four white men are at a place a short way from here, just before the flatland country opens up. They came from the direction of Cheyenne and Blue Dog says they are waiting in ambush for someone.'

'An ambush?'

'That's what he said,' Daniel replied. 'He understands a little English and heard one say to be ready, that *the hunter* would be coming.'

'It can't be the men we're after lying in wait for us,' Lucas argued. 'How would they know I survived and that we were coming this way?'

'Jim Grogan knows you're alive,' Daniel pointed out. 'He knows we are going to look for the two men who dry-gulched you.'

'Grogan isn't behind the robbery. I've known him for years. He's about as honest as they come.'

'I suppose the livery man might have passed word to them,' Daniel said. 'He seemed straightforward enough, but they might have paid him to let them know if anyone came asking.'

'Would have made more sense to pay him to tell anyone they went to Denver.'

'It's possible the trap is for someone else,' Daniel said. 'How do you want to proceed, partner?'

'We'll do this careful-like, being there are four men. You're more experienced in this kind of thing — what's the best way for us to sneak up and take a look?'

'The best way would be for you to stay here and wait for me' — he quickly held up a hand — 'but I know that isn't going to happen.'

'I won't stay behind, but I am willing to follow your lead.'

'Iris will like that,' Daniel teased Lucas, 'you being willing to follow orders.'

Lucas withdrew his Henry rifle and levered a round into the chamber. 'Let's get moving.'

Blue Dog had given Daniel a good idea of the approximate position of the waiting men. After riding a short distance, they stopped the horses and dismounted in a thicket of scrub brush. It was high enough to conceal their animals from view, so they tied them off and continued on foot.

Lucas had hunted all of his life and knew how to be quiet, while Daniel had been with the Indians for a good many years. The pair moved soundlessly forward, circling a hill, cautious not to be detected before discovering what lay ahead.

'Smell that?' Daniel barely breathed the words as they neared the ridge.

'Cigarette smoke,' Lucas replied in an equally soft whisper, catching a faint whiff.

They hunkered down and crept up behind a sprawling sagebrush. From their elevated position, they looked and listened for any movement. After five full minutes, Daniel pointed to a man, nearly concealed between two rocks and a stand of dead grass. Lucas nodded and indicated the one with the cigarette. They both had rifles and appeared to be watching the trail. Moments later, they spied two more hiding down near the trail — men readily identifiable to Lucas — Buck and Whitey!

'I'll be damned!' Lucas muttered softly. 'It's the back-shooters, sure enough. I can't figure how they knew I was alive and we'd come this way.'

'Hard to say how they learned you

were alive, but this is the shortest and safest route from Tolberg's place to Cheyenne.'

'Your having been a member of Ghost Bull's tribe sure came in handy. If you hadn't talked to those scouts, we would have ridden right into a trap.'

'Never liked Blue Dog all that much before,' Daniel said. 'He and I had eyes for the same young maiden — she chose him.'

'Smart girl,' Lucas teased.

'Thanks,' Daniel replied drily. 'What's the plan now?'

'The horses are tethered on a picket rope,' Lucas pointed out. 'Four horses . . . four men. Blue Dog was right about their number.'

'I can get to the one with the cigarette without being seen or heard. Can you reach the other one, the guy nearest the horses?'

'So long as I don't have to crawl very far,' Lucas told him truthfully. 'I'm not sure my mending is complete enough for me to get too strenuous.'

'Great, I've got to babysit you through a battle and we're facing two-to-one odds.'

Lucas gave him a playful poke in the shoulder. 'You get your man — I'll get mine.'

Daniel moved away, slithering between the bushes as silently as a snake. Lucas had to proceed carefully, so as not to jar his injury more than necessary. His legs were in good shape so he crouched low and duck-walked a short way. Then he used mostly his stronger arm and continued by doing a three-legged sort of crawl, keeping his rifle tucked in against his chest with his free hand.

The tethered horses naturally shifted their stance, stomped to ward off gnats or flies, and made other noises while munching the nearby foliage. Their sounds covered what little noise Lucas made during his movements.

At a position some thirty feet from the guard, Lucas picked up a pebble and waited until the man was staring down at the trail. When the ambusher shifted his attention in that direction, Lucas tossed the small stone and hit one of the horses right between the ears. The animal spooked, jerked back on the picket line and snorted. The man whirled about to see what had caused the disturbance.

Lucas rose up and covered the distance in several long strides. The sound of his approach warned the guard at the last instant. As the man spun about, Lucas swung the rifle like a club!

A flash of surprise and shock sprang into the man's face. At the same instant the rifle barrel slammed against his skull. Too slow to fend off the attack, the guard, a reasonably young man, crumpled to the ground in an unconscious heap.

'Walt?' Buck's voice called out, having heard the disturbance. 'Sing out! What's happening up there?'

Quickly binding the man's hands behind him, Lucas had no idea what the man's voice sounded like. He held his silence and hoped Daniel had been able to reach his man. If not, there still might be three gunmen to deal with.

'Skyler!' Buck shouted a second time. 'You in position?'

No answer.

'It's Lucas or Injuns!' Whitey told Buck. 'Do we fight or run?'

'They've got the horses,' Buck snarled the reply. 'We got no choice.'

Reasonably certain Daniel had taken care of the man called Skyler, Lucas eased forward to a better position, then called out to the two remaining men.

'I'm giving you boys a choice,' he shouted. 'You can toss out your shooting irons and surrender quietly, or you can die here today.' With an icy edge to his voice, 'That's more of a choice than you gave me.'

Having given away his approximate location, he eased a few feet along behind the brush, keeping the horses in sight. As long as he blocked their escape, Buck and Whitey's only choice was to fight or give up.

A bullet sang off a rock several feet away, followed quickly by two more shots — all striking the rocky ground inches from where he had been when he called out. The two killers were not green at this kind of fighting.

'It's no prison cell for us,' Buck yelled up at Lucas. 'You want our hides, you'll damn well earn the right to skin us!'

A rifle opened up from where the cigarette man had been waiting. Daniel made his presence known, but a quick peek around the edge of his cover told Lucas he had missed.

The shooting became sporadic, a muzzle flash here or there and then the sounds of men moving and changing positions. In a standoff such as this, the first one to make a mistake was going to be the first man to die.

Lucas was not in a good place. He was located above Whitey and Buck, but most of the terrain was higher around him. He was down in a slight hollow, where any attempt to move left

167

or right would expose him to the shooters below. He could retreat safely, but he would lose track of the animals. If he moved over near the horses, he would not be in a position to shoot at the two men.

As for Buck and Whitey, they had an abundance of cover — piñon, sage and scrub brush, along with a few sizable boulders and runoff ditches. They could easily maneuver about to one side or the other without exposing themselves to gunfire.

Lucas gave thought to the situation. It was only a matter of time before one of those men slipped away and worked up the hill to find a vantage point. If he stayed where he was, the shooter would be able to pick him off with an easy shot. The problem was, he had to keep watch on the cavvy of horses to prevent an escape. That responsibility limited his ability to take the fight to Buck and Whitey. Then he had a thought.

★　★　★

Whitey crawled over to Buck's side. Neither of them was the kind of man to panic or run from a fight. They had been in a number of scrapes before and had always got out with a whole skin.

'We can keep that second man pinned down,' Whitey said, tipping his head to where Skyler had been, 'But Lucas can circle us from above and get behind us.'

'Not without leaving the horses unguarded,' Buck informed him. 'He won't take that chance.'

'What if there are more than two of them?'

'They would have come in hard and fast if numbers had been on their side. They took out Skyler and Walt like a couple Indians.' He shook his head. 'No, there's only two — an even fight.'

'Them being the odds, Buck, it gives me an idea for getting the upper hand.'

'What's your idea?' Buck asked.

'You keep the one guy pinned and toss a round up toward Lucas now and again. I'm going to slip out the back door and circle the hill. I can come up behind him.'

'What makes you think he'll stay put?'

'Like you said, he has to mind the horses so we can't grab a mount and make a run for it. That means he'll stay high enough on the rim of the ridge to see both the horses and down into the hollow. I can sneak out the back way, because there's plenty of cover and it doesn't appear to lead anywhere. They won't be expecting it.'

Buck took a moment to load his rifle. Whitey did the same.

'You use both guns,' Whitey said, when he had his rifle ready. 'It'll make them think both of us are still down here together.'

'Go get that die-hard son,' Buck told his cohort, 'and let's make damn sure the man is dead this time!'

Whitey displayed an evil smirk. 'I'll look him square in the face as I watch the light go out of his eyes!'

Buck fired off a round at the man

who had eliminated Skyler. A moment later, he took a shot up the hill with Whitey's gun, shooting toward the last place he had seen Lucas. Whitey had moved with the first blast and was already out of sight.

'Must have been an angel riding on your shoulder the day we left you for dead, Lucas,' Buck muttered. 'Well, you won't be coming back from the grave a second time.'

Whitey moved like a wisp of smoke in a strong breeze. He retreated rearward a full hundred yards before he began to circle. He had hunted every kind of animal there was and also a fair number of Indians. He knew how to stalk his prey.

The late spring sun beat down, but it was not overly hot. Wyoming seldom got above the ninety-degree mark even in midsummer. Of course there was a strong breeze wafting through the hills. Whitey thought the state should have been named Windoming, giving credit to the fact the wind always seemed to blow.

Once to the perimeter of the nearby foothill, Whitey began to work his way upward. He knew where the horses were at, so he threaded a path in that direction. Lucas would have to be in a position to watch the mounts, so it only allowed him to move a short way along the ridge. Whitey pulled his skinning knife and felt a glow of confidence. He would sneak up behind the slippery son and put an end to his miserable life.

Nearing the summit of the hill, he used the thick brush for concealment and soundlessly inched forward. His eyes searched the area, seeking movement, while listening for any whisper of noise not connected to the breeze. Lucas had to be near the lip of the rim and his back would be to Whitey. With a growing assurance, he skirted a short distance below the hillock's crest, taking a direction which would allow him to step right in behind the man. One fatal stab of the blade and it would be the end of Lucas. Whitey eased up over the ridge, positioned right where he needed to be to see both Lucas and the horses —

He stopped dead still and stared. It couldn't be! The horses were gone!

★ ★ ★

Lucas could have covered Whitey with his gun, but the man would have probably charged at him. Both killers knew a noose or many years in a prison awaited them if they surrendered. These two desperadoes would die before giving up their freedom.

Lucas set the rifle down and reached up behind the back of his neck. His hand grasped the handle of his Bowie knife and he pulled it from its sheath.

'Looking for me, Whitey?' he asked.

The man whirled about. He obviously expected Lucas to be holding a gun. When he spied the knife, he displayed a sneer.

'After being shot a couple weeks back, I'm surprised you would have the guts to take me on in a fair fight, Lucas.'

'It's more than a back-shooter like you deserves.'

Whitey came forward, slowly sweeping his knife blade back and forth, loosening his muscles for the coming battle. Lucas recognized this was a man who knew how to fight.

However, Lucas had grown up listening to his father tell tales of Jim Bowie, the greatest knife fighter who ever lived. The story of when Bowie had been attacked by three men — and he killed them all with his big knife — was one he had never grown tired of hearing. His father had worked long hours to teach him the art of knife fighting, using carved wooden knives for practice from the time he could walk. With Whitey thinking Lucas would be stiff and sore from his wound, he figured to have the advantage. It showed in his approach.

Whitey came at him like an Indian, balanced on his toes, making quick, darting jabs with the edge of the blade up so it could rip his opponent apart once inserted deep into the flesh. But Lucas was quick and read his every move. He dodged back from Whitey a time or two, staying just out of reach, watching his opponent and studying his fighting style.

After patiently circling twice, Lucas went on the attack. He feigned two quick moves — one a slashing movement and the other, a backhand swing using the handle as a club.

Whitey jerked back, then quickly reacted to try and block the second lunge. It was a mistake —

Instead of following through with the vicious swat, Lucas reversed his motion and drove the deadly blade forward. Whitey was already moving. He couldn't shift his weight fast enough to jump back and the large knife found its mark. It penetrated deep into his side and the breath was ripped from his lungs like a punctured balloon. He grunted in shock as his life deserted its body. Mere seconds after the fight had begun Whitey lay dead on the ground.

Lucas bent at the middle, sucking air slowly, so as not to induce any added pain to his still mending wound. Before he recovered enough to call out to Buck and tell him to surrender, that he was now alone, a single shot rang out. He held his breath until he heard Daniel shout, 'I got him!'

Lucas hurried to the rim, but remained cautious about lifting his head where he might be silhouetted against the sky. His concern was for naught. Daniel was striding down the hill, convinced his bullet had finished off the second killer.

Lucas made his way down the hill to join him, and he spotted Buck lying on his face. The shot had caught him high in the neck and probably killed him instantly.

'Damn it all, Daniel,' he complained, 'I wanted him alive.'

Daniel reached the body first and turned him over with his foot. 'Dead as a rock,' he declared. 'You should have told me we needed him to be able to talk.'

'Yeah, I can see that now.'

'This fellow was trying to make us think there were two men down here,' Daniel explained. 'He kept firing one shot in my direction, then a second or two later, he changed rifles and would rear up and fire at where he thought you were. I figured out his little act and, when he reared up, I popped him like a wild turkey.'

'I wanted to ask him some questions,' Lucas repeated.

'It's not my fault,' Daniel complained. 'I can't help it if I made a good shot.'

'Did you kill the smoker too?'

'Uh.' Daniel shrugged his shoulders. 'You never said not to.' Then he tipped his head toward the ridge. 'How about the other hired killer?'

'Whitey,' Lucas told him the man's name. 'I moved the horses down to where we left our own. Whitey figured I had to be on the ridge, so I got behind him when he came to ambush me.'

'I didn't hear a gunshot.'

'No, we settled things like a couple barbarians.'

'So I'm to blame for killing Buck, while you sent Whitey to hell in a wheelbarrow?'

'All right, I suppose you have a point.' Daniel laughed. 'What now?'

'Unlike you, I didn't *kill* the man guarding the horses. You go get the animals and bring them here while I fetch him. Maybe he can tell us something.'

Walt was willing to talk, but mostly to complain about his headache. Plus he seemed to know very little about Whitey and Buck. He had come along because Skyler was his cousin and promised him an easy fifty dollars.

'How did they know we would be coming this way?' Daniel asked.

'I don't know nothing about it,' Walt lamented. 'I was only supposed to watch the horses.'

'You were part of an ambush set up to kill two men,' Lucas told him sternly. 'Don't tell me you didn't ask some questions!'

'Skyler told me I wouldn't have to do nothing but watch the horses,' he whined the reply. 'I only heard the one called Buck saying they should have asked for more money.'

Lucas glanced at Daniel, who returned the look with interest.

'We have to finish our trip to Cheyenne,' Lucas told Daniel. 'We can turn in the bodies to the law there and see if anyone can shed a little more light on our two killers.'

'If they said something about asking for more money, that means they have an accomplice,' Daniel agreed. 'I went through the saddle-bags from their horses and checked the pockets of our four bushwhackers. They don't have a hundred dollars between them.'

'Let's pack them on their horses and get moving. With luck, we can make Cheyenne by dark.'

'That's pushing it, but once we hit the main trail we can keep riding until we get there.'

'How about me?' Walt asked. 'I didn't

shoot at you boys.'

Lucas didn't bother to argue that he would have, if not for being unconscious! Instead, he said, 'It'll be up to the law in Cheyenne as to what happens to you.'

'Easy money!' Walt spat on the ground and threw an angry look at his cousin's body. 'If you wasn't dead, Skyler, I'd whup the daylights out of you!'

9

The marshal, Curly Carlson, appeared younger than Lucas by a year or two, but he seemed a fair judge of character. After listening to what Lucas, Daniel and their prisoner had to say, he took charge of the situation.

'Bernie!' he commanded a gent who looked old enough to have voted for George Washington as President, 'Put Walt here in the cell and then go tell Saul we've got three bodies for him.'

'Sure thing,' the aged gent said, putting his attention on the ambusher. 'Get your carcass into that there cell, sonny boy,' he directed Walt. 'I'll 'spect you to talk kindly to me and do exactly as I says, 'cause I'm the one who brings your meals.'

Walt didn't offer any argument, but went quietly into the first of the two cells.

'How are you going to go about getting more information?' Curly asked.

'Those men must have been staying here in town. We'd like to see their room and then talk to the banker.'

'You think they might have hidden or stashed the payroll they stole somewhere close by?'

Lucas displayed a curious frown. 'I don't think Buck and Whitey were in the robbery alone. Someone tipped them we were coming.'

'And they weren't carrying a lot of money on them,' Daniel added.

'I'd venture a good place to stop is at the telegraph office,' Curly suggested. 'Mort can tell us if those fellows or any other strangers in town have been getting news or messages.'

'He would probably be more inclined to talk with you involved, Marshal,' Lucas pointed out.

'Let's go see what we can find out,' the young man volunteered.

★ ★ ★

Iris heard a horse enter the yard and hurried to look out the window. Her heart sank at seeing a stranger. It had been two weeks and there had not been a word from Lucas. She hated not knowing if he had been hurt in a fight or been killed while trying to bring those robbers to justice. How long was a girl supposed to wait? Was she supposed to put her life in a box and leave it closed up tight until a month had passed? Several months? A year?

The man climbed down stiffly from his horse. Attired in a suit and rather fashionable felt business hat, he seemed sorely out of place so far from the nearest city. He tied off his mount at the hitching post, then paused to place his hands on his hips and slowly arch his back.

'Long ride?' she asked, moving to the open doorway.

A professional smile rushed to his face, another clue that this man was used to dealing with customers or social peers. He doffed his hat and Iris noticed that his hair was neatly groomed, as was his mustache.

'I hail from Crossbow, dear lady,' he said, displaying immediate warmth in his personality. 'It is at the behest of a close friend that I made the journey to your fair trading post. Might I get a cup of coffee and something to eat here?'

'We brew fresh coffee every morning — not the huckleberry or woodchip sort, but from real coffee beans.'

'Ah, there is civilization beyond the borders of Crossbow,' he praised. 'I'm Jim Grogan, and I have no doubt you are Iris Ducane.'

The statement caused Iris to stare. 'I've heard your name before. You hired Lucas to take a payroll to a mine in the Black Hills!'

There was no smile now. 'Biggest mistake of my life,' Jim admitted gravely. 'Nearly got him killed and it was all my fault.'

'Why are you here?' she asked. 'Lucas is off to God-knows-where, searching for the men who tried to kill him.'

'For a cup of coffee and something to eat, I will tell you all I know.'

'Iris hesitated, not wanting to wait for any information about Lucas. However, she decided five or ten minutes would not make much difference.'

'We didn't prepare anything special for meals today, but I have biscuits and gravy, plus some wild currant pie. It's four-bits in cash or trade.'

'Sounds like a feast, after the miles I've traveled,' Jim said.

Hank heard the talking and came in from the back, where he had been cleaning some hides for tanning. Jim introduced himself while the three of them sat down for lunch. Her uncle and Jim conversed mostly about the major battle brewing in the Black Hills. Both men expected there would be a long and bloody war before the trouble was settled. When the meal was over, Iris cleared away the dishes and then confronted Jim.

'You said you had something to say to me,' she stated firmly. 'That's your second cup of coffee and I've waited until — '

Jim laughed and tipped his head at her uncle. 'I wasn't stringing you along, madam,' he said amiably. 'I thought you might prefer to hear this privately.'

Hank snorted and rose from the table. 'I been waiting for it,' he said testily. 'Allow a woman in the house and suddenly there's all kinds of secrets.' He picked up his hat from a nearby peg on the wall. 'If you need me, I'll be out whittling me a toothpick or mending the corral. Sure wouldn't want to be snooping over something where my nose don't belong.'

'Thank you, Uncle,' Iris said.

She waited until he went out the front door before she whirled on Jim. 'Now give!' she demanded. 'What do you have to tell me?'

'First off, Lucas and Daniel are both fine,' he began. 'Lucas sent me a telegram from Cheyenne.' He removed a piece of paper from his pocket and began to read the printing.

'Jim, job will take longer than expected. Please get word to Iris Ducane that I will return as soon as I can. It's important. Signed Lucas.'

Iris regarded him with a wondrous stare. 'You rode all the way from Crossbow just to read me the telegraph message?'

'Lucas said it was important,' he said, as if that was a completely satisfactory answer. He showed a smile again, but this time it was genuine, not professional. 'I can see why he is concerned. I'll bet you have a host of admirers chasing after you.'

She felt a warmth creep up into her cheeks. 'There aren't many single white women in this part of the country.'

'Lucas has been a friend of mine for many years, Miss Ducane. It's true, I was his boss, but he isn't the sort of guy you have to tell to do anything. If something needs doing, he sees the job gets done.'

'He did strike me as being capable,' she agreed. 'Plus, the first time I met him he had rescued an Indian woman and her child from death.'

'That's his nature,' Jim said. 'Rarely does someone meet a person they can trust with their very life. Lucas is such a man.'

'I appreciate your coming all this way.' She was sincere. 'To tell the truth, I had begun to worry about Lucas. I expected him back by now.'

'Precisely the reason I made the trip from Crossbow,' Jim said. He paused to hand her a silver dollar. 'For the coffee, meal and pie,' he said. 'I believe it will hold me until I get back to town.'

'This is too much — you rode all this way — you shouldn't pay for — '

Jim shook his head. 'No, no, dear girl,' he cut her off. 'I made the ride here for Lucas. You don't owe me anything and the currant pie was worth the trip. You're a fine cook.'

Not knowing what else to say, Iris followed the man out of the trading post and waited while he climbed aboard his horse. He said a short farewell and turned back in the direction he had come.

Hank appeared, having obviously been trying to eavesdrop from the side of the house. He walked over to stand at her side as Jim was lost beyond the trees.

'He tell you what you wanted to hear?' he asked somewhat stuffily.

'Lucas won't be back for a while yet.'

'Then he didn't tell you what you wanted to hear,' Hank grumbled. 'Guess that means you're going to keep on moping about like someone sat on your birthday cake.'

'I'm not as bad as all that.'

'Who was it gave me hell for putting away the dish I used after cleaning that there rabbit I shot yesterday?'

'You didn't even wash off the blood!' she cried.

Hank ducked his head and muttered, 'I wiped it off with a rag.'

'I'm not going to eat or serve something on a plate that's covered with blood smears!' she declared. 'And it makes no difference whether I was concerned about Lucas or not.'

'It makes a difference in how you strip the bark from my hide,' he lamented. 'Time before or two that I done the same thing, you called me on it and that was it. This time, you like to tore my head off.'

'I'm sorry if I was unduly critical, Uncle,' she apologized. 'Next time I'll simply use the bloody bowl or dish to serve up your porridge!'

'See?' his voice rose an octave. 'That there is what I'm talking about. You done turned into a nagging, hard-case shrew.'

Iris heaved an audible sigh. 'I've got laundry to do, Uncle.'

'Probably rub all the thread out of the material,' he grumbled again. 'I been saying it all my life, females is nothing but trouble.'

★　★　★

Gil Martin arrived at his luxurious hotel room — high-faluting sorts called it a suite — shortly after midnight, turned up the wall lamp and closed the door to the hallway. He wore an expensive suit and top hat, and smelled of toilet water, the kind a fancy barber would sometimes splash on a man after a shave.

'You seem to be doing pretty well for a man who went broke a few weeks back,' Lucas spoke from a shadowy corner of the room.

Daniel stepped out from a clothes closet to block the door swiftly. He pointed a pistol at Martin and put a finger to his lips to remain quiet.

'Who are you?' Martin snapped the question at Daniel. 'What are you two ruffians doing in my room?'

'I've got sixteen thousand reasons for being here,' Lucas told him, moving into the light. 'Add one more if you count being shot and left for dead.'

'Two more,' Daniel corrected. 'Let's not forget about the ambush.'

The haughty pretense drained from the man's face, along with all other hint of color. His eyes grew wide and fearful, darting quickly about the room like those of a trapped animal.

'Played us all for fools, didn't you, Martin — if that's your real name,' Lucas said. 'Put up insurance money on a make-believe mine and collect the difference when you fake a robbery and kill the only innocent man in the group.'

'Listen to me,' he began to plead, 'I was forced to do it! Those two killers, Buck and Whitey, it was their plan. I wanted no part of it!'

'We checked the finances of those two, after we laid them to rest in a beggars' field, next to the cemetery,' Daniel was the one to speak. 'All their cash and worth combined, along with what they paid their two hired thugs, didn't amount to three hundred dollars.'

'Plus, you wired those two we were coming, after Grogan contacted you to tell you I was alive and we were tracking the two robbers.'

'I don't know what you're talking about,' he whined. 'I told you, it was them! They forced me to go along with it their scheme for a thousand dollars. That's all I have!'

Daniel removed his hat and allowed his hair to fall about his shoulders. He removed his yellow head band and put it on. Then he removed his shirt, displaying his dark, tanned skin and well-muscled physique.

'Daniel is half-Cheyenne,' Lucas told Martin in a matter-of-fact tone of voice. 'I asked him to let me reason with you, but there's a war going on between the soldiers and the Indians. Men like you are a big reason for that war — seeking gold in the Black Hills, after it was given to the Indians. Men like you make it necessary for the soldiers to protect prospectors and settlers, in the name of greed.'

'Look, I'm telling you, this wasn't my idea. Buck and Whitey — '

Daniel pulled his skinning knife and moved forward.

Martin's frightened gaze went from the knife to Lucas. 'Wait a minute!' he cried. 'We can work something out.'

'This white man steals from the Indian and he steals from his own kind,' Daniel said, snarling like an angry dog. 'I will take your hair and decorate my teepee!'

'Lucas!' Martin was practically blubbering, backing away from Daniel until he hit the wall. 'You've got to help me! I can make this right!'

'Sorry, but I can't help you,' Lucas remained passive. 'You're only a small-time swindler, one who was hired to rob a bank and kill a courier. Can't expect us to respect some little fish like you.'

Daniel leapt forward, using his forearm against Martin's neck to pin him to the wall. He eyed the man's hair again.

'Nice of you to wash that scalp,' he sneered. 'Saves me the trouble of doing anything more than rinsing off the blood!'

'No-o-o-o!' Martin wailed. 'Help me, Lucas!'

'I kind of promised him a scalp,' Lucas replied, lifting his shoulders in a shrug. 'We didn't get a chance with Buck and Whitey, so you'll have to do.'

'Wait!' Martin cried again, terrified that Daniel would start cutting. 'I'll tell you the truth! I can get back the money! I'll do anything you want!'

★　★　★

Jim Grogan was all smiles. He shook the hands of Daniel and Lucas, then shook them a second time.

'I never thought you'd do it,' he said. 'You're the best man I ever knew, Lucas, but I didn't think you could ever get the bank's money back.'

'I couldn't have done it without Daniel.'

'Yes, yes, I'm deeply indebted to you both.'

'Seems Martin and his pals had pulled this stunt a time or two before.' Lucas told him what they had learned. 'Martin — his real name is Hanley

— would find someone to invest in a mine or some other business venture and then figure a way to steal their money.'

'It was a first-rate act by all three of them,' Jim said. 'I believed every word they told me . . . and I've encountered a few crooks before.'

'They were good,' Lucas agreed. 'I didn't suspect a thing right up until the moment they shot me in the back. If not for Daniel here, the three of them would probably be planning another job together.'

Jim reached out and shook Daniel's hand again — for the third time. 'I can't tell you men how much this helps my position here. I was borderline after losing the money and there was talk about possibly closing the bank. At the very least, I would be walking a narrow beam for a good many years — one misstep and my career would have been over.'

'Fourteen thousand dollars,' Lucas told .him, reminding him of the bank draft from Denver. I reckon that makes you come out right where you expected when you decided to insure the payroll.'

'Yes, but I owe you . . . '

'We already got our share,' Lucas said. 'We had no way of tracking down the men Martin swindled before — he used a different name for every job — and the marshal assured us he wouldn't be needing all that much money while he was serving twenty years in prison.'

'Well, I still feel I owe you something.'

'Did you do the little chore I asked?' Lucas wanted to know.

A wide smile revealed Jim still had most of his teeth. 'That Iris is a sweet little thing, Lucas. She seemed real eager to know what you were up to.'

'Yeah, I'm heading that way soon as we leave here.'

'One other thing,' he grew deadly serious. 'Don't know if you have heard or not, but there was a big fight back in the Black Hills . . . a place called the

Little Big Horn. Some general named Custer and near two hundred soldiers were killed. The report says the general led his men into a trap and they ended up facing several thousand Indians. They are calling it a massacre.'

Lucas felt a great sadness enter his being. 'That will be the end of the Indian way of life,' he predicted. 'The army will bring however men it takes to squash the different tribes. It won't end until every Indian is on a reservation or dead.'

'Custer's men still carried single-shot carbines,' Jim said. 'Doubt it would have made much difference against such overwhelming odds, but with those antiquated guns, they had no chance.'

Daniel looked over at Lucas. There was pain in his eyes, but he suffered his inner agony and turmoil in silence. When he spoke, there was a dread conviction in his voice.

'I think it would be wise to visit a barber, Lucas.'

'Yes, my friend, the choice of red or white has been made for you. There's no going back now.'

'Hell!' Jim exclaimed, 'If Lucas hadn't told me you were half-Cheyenne, I'd have never guessed it. You're not much darker than Lucas and you talk as good as me.'

'My father wanted me to be educated,' Daniel replied.

The two of them started for the door, but Jim hurried over and shook their hands a last time. 'I'm wishing you boys luck' — with a wink — 'and, Lucas, I hope you invite me to the wedding.'

'Got to get back to that girl before she up and marries someone else,' Lucas replied back. 'Soon as we get something to eat and a few hours of sleep, we'll be pulling out and heading for Tolberg's place.'

'*And* after I get my hair cut,' Daniel reminded him.

Lucas grinned. 'Sounds like a good idea for us both.'

10

'*Quoi*? I don't understand what you're saying,' Philippe complained, displaying a complete lack of comprehension. 'You are telling me you prefer an unkempt, boorish, vagabond hunter to a respectable officer and gentleman of polite society such as myself?'

'See?' Iris was blunt, 'You *do* understand.'

'But the man is a rogue, a scoundrel, a wandering nomad without a home or capital to his name. Do you wish to end up living the life of a savage, to become a white squaw?' He titled his nose upward in a show of contempt. '*Non*, even the lowest Indian will have a place on a reservation — you will have nothing!'

'You asked me to give you my decision,' Iris replied. 'I gave it to you.'

'But you are mad! Totally mad!'

Philippe ranted.

The sound of approaching horses turned their attention to the new arrivals. Iris felt a lightness enter her being and her heart leapt in delight.

'Lucas!' she shouted happily. 'He's back!'

★ ★ ★

'Looks like trouble,' Daniel told Lucas, at their advance. 'It's that French-Creole captain, Philippe Bagot.'

'I didn't realize you knew him?'

'Uh, we've had our differences. He knows more about me than I'd like.'

Lucas rode up to the corral and dismounted. Daniel followed suit and then took the reins of both horses.

Captain Bagot stormed over to confront Lucas. He stopped a few feet away and bared his teeth like a snarling dog. 'You ride with a collaborator!' he cried. 'I will see you hanged for this, Monsieur Lucas, you traitorous dog!'

'That would be *Mister* Lucas, if you

don't mind,' Lucas replied with a purposeful calm.

'Of course,' Philippe was sarcastic. 'You obviously hate the French.'

'Only one of them,' Lucas corrected. He showed a smirk. 'Care to guess which one?'

'Jest if you like, but I will have you both arrested and hauled away in irons!'

Lucas looked at the captain, then glanced over at his half-dozen men. They were sitting in the shade a short way from the trading post, few showing much interest over their fearless leader's ire.

'I've committed no crime, Bagot,' Lucas argued, 'And you can't hang a man for siding with his own people. Daniel belongs to the Cheyenne tribe and was following orders from his superior, Ghost Bull.'

'He is not an Indian!'

'His mother is a cousin to Pretty Bird, Ghost Bull's wife. You can't bring charges against him for doing what he was told.'

'If that is true, I shall have him placed into custody and transferred to the nearest reservation!'

'I hired him to ride with me after he saved my life. It was also his people who warned us that we were about to ride into an ambush a couple weeks back. You'll not be placing him under arrest while I'm here.'

Bagot's expression was sheer hatred. 'You come here and turn my woman against me,' he hissed vehemently, 'and now you ride with one of the men responsible for the massacre at Little Big Horn. I will not let this pass without some form of retribution.'

Lucas took a moment to glance at Iris. She was out of earshot but lifted her shoulders in a shrug. It told him what he needed to know.

'Oh, I see the problem now,' he told Bagot. 'Your feelings were hurt when Iris told you she was in love with me.'

The instant rush of color to his already rage-darkened face revealed the truth of that statement. 'I am going to arrest your half-Indian friend and see to it he never knows another day of true freedom.'

'No need to pick on him when it's me you want to fight.'

Bagot did not deny it. 'If we were in Louisiana, and I was not an officer in the military, I would challenge you to a duel and leave you dying in the dirt!'

'I've heard a little about those affairs of honor,' Lucas said. 'What does it take to start something like that?'

'It is usually the swat of a glove to your opponent's cheek,' Philippe answered. 'But I am forbidden by my uniform to challenge anyone.'

Lucas launched a right hand and punched the captain flush in the jaw. It was hard enough that it knocked him off balance. He landed on his backside with a grunt, both shocked and dazed.

'I don't have a glove handy,' Lucas explained why he had hit him. 'Will that do?'

Bagot sat upright, consumed with fury. 'You dare to challenge me!'

'For Daniel's freedom,' Lucas replied. 'You win — you take him into custody. I win — you ride out and forget you ever knew his name.'

The soldiers had been relaxed, even with their captain shouting in a rage. Seeing him knocked to the ground, it brought them running — not to his aid, but to see what would happen next. Lucas got the impression Captain Bagot was something of a pompous autocrat around his men and not all that popular. Some of them appeared more than pleased at seeing him knocked down a peg.

Iris also rushed over. 'Lucas!' she cried. 'What are you doing?'

'You are a fool,' Bagot said, ignoring Iris while getting to his feet. 'As you have challenged me, I am the one who selects the weapon of choice.'

'Guns, knives, fists, clubs . . . makes no difference to me.'

Bagot showed a satisfied smile. 'I choose swords!'

'No!' Iris cried. 'That isn't fair!'

But Lucas waved off her concern. 'Fine by me,' he accepted the choice. 'When and where?'

Bagot lifted his chin, displaying a confident air of superiority. 'Ten minutes — right on this very spot.'

'Ten minutes is fine, I need to wash off some of this trail dust and get a drink of water first.'

Iris moved over and grabbed hold of his arm. 'Are you insane, Lucas?' she cried. 'He will cut you up like a Thanksgiving turkey! He has bragged to me about how he has injured or killed a number of men in duels.'

Lucas dismissed her concern. 'He never took on a hunter or mountain man before, Bright Eyes. I'll be all right.'

Daniel had come over to join them. He also had a worried look on his face. 'If you get yourself killed, do I have to follow through on your promise?'

'It was my word, not your own,' Lucas told him, keeping his voice low. 'If he kills me, I'd appreciate your doing the same to him.'

The words caused Daniel to grin. 'That sounds better.'

'Let's hope you don't have to do anything but pat me on the back after this is over.'

'It won't be as much fun, but I'll go along with that.'

'Lucas, I — ' Iris began.

'Let me clean up and get a drink of water,' he prevented her from voicing more concern. 'You and Daniel find a place in the shade to watch. I'll be fine.'

The two of them stood back as he went to the watering trough and began to rinse the dust from his face and hands. Hank came out to speak to him while he was there.

'That Cajun or Creole — whatever kind of Frenchman he is — he might prance about like a peacock with his tail spread, but I'll wager he knows how to use a sword.'

'I see you've got some hides drying on the side of the shed.'

Hank frowned. 'Yeah, so what?'

207

'I need a thick piece of hide, the toughest stuff you've got.' At Hank's surprised look, he added, 'and bring me a couple strips of rawhide too.'

Hank hastened to do as he asked, while Lucas went inside the trading post and picked out a pair of heavy leather gloves. He knew he had no chance against the captain with an actual sword, but he didn't figure the man would refuse to let him use the weapon of his own choosing. After all, Iris was part of the audience and he wouldn't want to look weak in front of his men.

Hank arrived a couple minutes later and Lucas had him help bind a thick piece of buffalo skin to his left wrist and palm with the rawhide strips. He then put on the thick left glove and flexed his fingers.

'That ought to do,' he said, admiring his handiwork. 'If I damage the glove, I'll buy it.' Hank's frown remained in place. 'Don't know what you have in mind, but you're sure enough going to keep one hand warm during this here contest.'

Lucas walked back to the clearing near the corral. Daniel and Iris were standing over next to the troopers, all awaiting the life and death duel. When Iris gave him an imploring look, he winked at her.

'I regret we cannot proceed,' Bagot announced, his voice laced with disappointment. 'You have no sword and my men are carrying only carbines on this patrol.'

Lucas shook his head. 'I wasn't going to use a regular sword anyhow, Captain.' He reached up behind his neck and withdrew the Bowie knife from the scabbard. 'This here is my weapon of choice.'

'A knife?' Bagot snickered his disdain. 'You can't be serious!'

'I admit it gives me the advantage, but I figured you would want to be fair-minded about this here duel. I've never fought with a sword, but I do know a little about knife fighting.'

'You heard the man, Bagot!' Daniel called out. 'It's a fair fight, except his sword is a little shorter than yours.'

'That's right, Captain,' one of the soldiers encouraged. 'He's the one who claims to have an equal chance. Let him try!'

Several more of the troopers began to shout for the fight to begin. Oddly enough, Lucas was pretty sure most of them were pulling for him!

The captain lifted his chin and drew his saber. 'Killing you won't be the challenge I had hoped, but I will have my satisfaction.'

'We going to chew the fat or get this here duel under way?' Lucas taunted.

Bagot approached with a military correctness, saluted with his sword, then lowered it to an attack position. He did not the make the mistake of underestimating Lucas, but began to circle, intermittently swishing the sword in a back and forth motion.

Lucas was poised in a knife-fighter's crouch, his weight evenly distributed, gloved hand extended to guard his left side, while the huge knife was ready in his right hand. He moved enough to remain facing Bagot, waiting for the moment to strike.

Bagot attacked as a swordsman, the blade making a quick arc as it slashed through the air within an inch of Lucas's chest. He retreated to avoid a reverse swipe of the sword and deflected a lunging jab with the blade of his knife.

The captain was quick, taking a half-dozen ferocious slices with his blade, attacking Lucas from right, left and front as smartly as an expert freighter with a short whip. He pressed the fight forward, driving Lucas back.

Retreating to avoid the long blade of his saber, Lucas parried the weapon with his knife and used his protected left hand and wrist to block two strikes from that side. He kept watching for the one moment when —

Bagot went flat-footed for an instant, making ready to shift his attack by changing the direction of his body. In that single instant Lucas sprang forward like a puma. His gloved left hand seized the sword by the blade and he yanked Bagot forward and off balance. At the same time, he brought his own knife inside the desperate grab of Bagot's free hand.

Lucas drove him several steps until he struck the corral fence. He pinned him there, knife against his throat, his gloved hand rendering Bagot's sword useless. With his jaw inches from the captain's shocked face, he rasped the next words in a bitter-cold tone of voice.

'This is how a knife fighter does it, Captain Bagot,' he threatened menacingly. 'One flick of my wrist and I will remove your head from your body!'

Bagot had no room to struggle or fight back, but he was a true duelist. 'You have the advantage,' he retorted a remarkably strong reply. 'I will not beg for mercy.'

Lucas relaxed his posture and stared the man square in the eyes. 'In an honorable fight, a real man doesn't beg ... but he can yield,' he told him quietly. 'I don't wish to kill you, Captain. Yield and allow Daniel to ride away a free man.'

The captain hesitated as if considering the offer. 'I am not a coward,' he said after a moment, 'but I will concede you have beaten me.'

'And Daniel?'

Bagot glanced over at the half-Cheyenne, dressed now like a white man, complete with his hair shorn as close to the scalp as any of the troopers. With a slight hint of humor in his voice, the captain replied, 'I seem to have forgotten anyone named Daniel Books.'

Lucas stepped back and withdrew his knife. When he released the sword with his left hand, he remained minimally cautious. It was unnecessary. The captain returned the sword to its scabbard, gave a curt nod to Lucas and rotated to address his men.

'Mount your horses!' he called out. 'We have some hard riding yet to do today and I will tolerate no stragglers under my command.'

As one, the troopers scrambled to get their horses. Bagot watched with approval and strode over to Iris.

'It would seem you have chosen the better man' — he lifted his chin — 'but only in the art of dueling. You are still making the mistake of your life in choosing Monsieur Lucas over me.'

Iris smiled. 'It's a choice I can live with, Philippe.'

The captain touched his hat in a salute and strode over to join his men. Within seconds they were gone, leaving behind only a lingering cloud of dust.

Hank helped Lucas remove the glove and thick piece of hide. Even with the protection, there were two minor gashes on his left arm. Iris hurried over at the sight of blood.

'You're hurt!' she cried.

'Only a scratch or two,' Lucas replied. 'The hide protected my wrist and palm for the most part.'

'I'll get my medical kit and patch you

up good as new,' Hank said, heading into the trading post.

Daniel took his cue from a single look from Lucas. 'Uh, I'll finish with the horses,' he said. 'Guess we'll have to buy one of the old nags from Hank before we can leave.'

'Leave?' Iris said, her attention lifting from the cuts on Lucas's arm to study his face. 'Leave to go where?'

'It isn't a good idea for Daniel to stick around in this neck of the woods, not after the massacre and all. We've a notion to settle down on the Colorado side of the border. It's where the three of us will start our ranch.'

'Three of us?' she feigned innocence. 'If you are including me, I haven't been asked.'

'You told Bagot you loved me — isn't that the truth?'

'No, I only told him I didn't love him.'

'Hmm, I hope you don't teach our kids to lie about something important like that.'

'Our kids?' she declared. 'You haven't

215

asked me to marry you yet. And what about after — how do we live?'

'As for how we will live, Daniel and I have a sizable amount of money to invest in our horse ranch. Concerning the marrying part . . . I think we ought to head straight for Crossbow. I kind of promised a friend he could attend the wedding.'

'That's about the poorest excuse for a proposal I can imagine!'

Lucas pulled her to him and kissed her. After a full minute, he released her so she could catch her breath. 'Marry me?' he asked gently.

She smiled. 'That's more like it, big boy.'

'I'll take that as a yes, Bright Eyes.'

''Bout damn time,' Hank snorted from the doorway. 'I been standing here five minutes waiting for you two to get that settled. Now get in here so I can tend to that arm!'

Lucas and Iris both laughed as they entered the trading post together hand-in-hand.

We do hope that you have enjoyed reading this large print book.

Did you know that all of our titles are available for purchase?

We publish a wide range of high quality large print books including:
**Romances, Mysteries, Classics
General Fiction
Non Fiction and Westerns**

Special interest titles available in large print are:
**The Little Oxford Dictionary
Music Book, Song Book
Hymn Book, Service Book**

Also available from us courtesy of Oxford University Press:
**Young Readers' Dictionary
(large print edition)
Young Readers' Thesaurus
(large print edition)**

For further information or a free brochure, please contact us at:
**Ulverscroft Large Print Books Ltd.,
The Green, Bradgate Road, Anstey,
Leicester, LE7 7FU, England.
Tel:** (00 44) **0116 236 4325**
Fax: (00 44) **0116 234 0205**

Other titles in the
Linford Western Library:

GUNS OF VIRTUE

Peter Wilson

Following the murder of his father, and his brother's decline into lawlessness, Adam Wade seeks revenge on the man he holds responsible. His search takes him to the town of Virtue, where ranch owner Hal Kember is a future state governor. But Adam becomes embroiled in a web of deceit and murder involving Kember's wife, Laura, his son, Luke, and a group of stage robbers and killers. In a final shootout there is one last life-changing shock for Adam.